I0598287

Lorde, Have Mercy

A Novel

By

Tikkia

Chapter 1

When I got to school this morning, I could barely get through the door before people started approaching me. Everyone was coming to me saying *"Mike Sinclair want you to meet him in the auditorium."*

Why? Nobody knew so, how could I? We had never spoken to one another. Only exchanged flirtatious glances. Mike is the guy that all the girls want a piece of. I'm not really sure why they fall all over him, but they do. He is cute, but not that cute. He's ai'ight. To me, Mike isn't that cute but, he is fly. I've never seen him wear anything twice, he keeps a fresh haircut and he always smells good. Well at least when we cross paths he does. Oh, and he has the most beautiful, contagious dimpled smile. He's not that cute, but he fits the description of cute. You know what I mean? Anyways, he's popular and he wanted to see me. I didn't know why he wanted to see me, but I was definitely going to find out. Being a freshman, I couldn't really afford not to go find out what he wanted. I mean I'm well liked but this could mean bigger things for my social status.

When I reached the auditorium, I could see him from the door. He had the attention of a small group and was telling them what seemed to be a gripping story. I decided to post up in the doorway to listen before going in. He was talking about his latest fling. He was 17 years old and already known for his flings. When I walked in, he was saying

"Yeah, so I was hittin' it real good from the back right? And she jumped off, threw me on the bed and started riding me like a champ. All of a sudden, her home-girl walked in, see she was stayin' the night over there. Anyway, she walked in but didn't walk back out. She was looking and when I looked over and saw her looking, I said 'fuck it sit on my face'" he said snapping his fingers and pointing to his mouth.

"That shit didn't happen" I said over the laughter that filled the air surrounding him. He turned his attention to me. I could tell that he didn't intend for me to hear his little story. He looked me up and down and back at my face, but our eyes didn't meet.

"No, not that last part, but it could have", he said finally looking me in the eye and   winking at me. "Hey Goddess, come on over here".

"My name is Lorde", I said approaching him.

"I know your name", he said smiling "Goddess suits you better", he stood up and gently touched my chin.

"No, Lorde does, but I see what you're trying to do there. That's cute" I said laughing at him in an attempt to hide the fact that I was actually blushing a little. I didn't have a crush on him, but my lady loins decided that they did, and his smile was not helping at all.

"Is that how you get the girls?" I ask returning the chin tap.

"Girls? What girls?" he said unable to keep from smiling again.

"Okay" I said nodding, "you can be cute one more time" I raised my index finger. I couldn't help it. I smiled too.

"Cute huh?" he said standing and wrapping me in his embrace. He didn't play sports, but he had broad shoulders and his arms were perfectly sculpted and they picked me up and hugged me tight. His body was rock hard, and he smelled delicious. I melted in his arms and when he put me down, I gave another squeeze to give myself an extra second to stabilize.

"What brings you around?" he asked with a smile that said he already knew why I was there.

"Well," I said, "I was walking by and I was so intrigued by the story of your latest rendezvous that I just had to stop in and listen. I especially like the part when you snapped your fingers and told her friend to sit on your face. I mean I was supposed to be meeting a guy name Mike here but you, you're much more interesting". He blushed a little.

"You weren't supposed to hear that" he said rubbing his head and looking around. Then, you could just see the lightbulb pop up before he said, "and it's a good thing I'm Mike", he wrinkled his forehead.

"Yeah right, I know who you are, and you know that so stop faking."

"Alright" he said rubbing his head again.

"I see you boo", I said noticing his waves and changing the subject, "Who needs a boat when you can make bitches seasick right here?" I said lightly smacking his hand down and running my own hand over his head. He burst into laughter.

"You a funny girl. I like that. I dig you Goddess."

"Well, I figured that much Mike. I'm here because you put the word out for me to meet you here. So" I shrug, "what's up?"

"Yeah, I put the word out because I wanted to talk to you. I keep seeing you around, but we never get a chance to talk."

"That's because I'm a freshman and you're a senior. I shouldn't be on your radar anyway."

"Why not? You don't exactly hang out with the rest of the freshman. You walk around with the upperclassmen like you own the joint and you're fine as hell and I think you might be in one of my classes" he shrugged, "you're on everyone's radar."

I don't have any classes with him, and he knows it. And I'm pretty sure I'm not on everyone's radar.

"So, what would you like to talk to me about?" I asked with a slight smirk, tilting my head to the side.

"I just wanted to know if I could get your phone number. Maybe we can get to know one another." He rocked back and forth nervously. I thought about it, but I didn't protest. I just gave it to him. He looked at me surprised, but he didn't say anything.

"I have to get to class, call me" I said and I walked away.

"Wait, let me walk you to class", he said jumping over a row of chairs to beat me to the door. I thought about it for a second and decided,

"No thank you but call me later." On my way to class I stopped by my locker.

"Hey girl", my friend Lola greeted me there. "I was looking for you. Where you been?"

"Well, damn near the whole school greeted me at the door about Mike. Where were you?"

"Wait, Mike? Mike who?" she asked, eyes getting wide as if she already knew the answer.

"You know which Mike. Mike Sinclair" I smiled.

"I knew it" she stomped "I missed it", she crossed her arms. I realized in that moment that she was just getting to school and she hadn't answered my question.

"Where have you been?" I asked

"Girl stop, with the two conversations at once thing. Focus. Mike Sinclair. What happened?"

"Oh nothing. He just wanted my phone number" I shrugged.

"Really Lorde? Only you can reduce the last 10 minutes to 10 seconds. You were just talking to the most popular guy in school. Bitches are about to want to be you. Do you know what this could do for your reputation?

There's a story there. Tell me", she demanded putting her hands on her hips.

"You know, if you were on time, you would've been there, so yes, ten minutes to ten seconds."

"Shut up girl. Did you give him your phone number?

"How do you do that? I ask disregarding her question.

"Do what?" She's getting annoyed with me now.

"Say so much without needing to take a breath?"

"Really Lorde? Really? Focus girl." I couldn't help but laugh.

"Did you give him your number?" She repeated her question and threw her hands up and let them fall. I knew I wasn't going to get out of this conversation. I tell Lola everything and this would be no different.

"Yeah I gave it to him" I said smiling.

"Yeah, I bet you did" she chuckled. "Like I said" she sang, "bitches are about to want to be you."

"Yeah right. I talk to Mike one time and what? He's my man now? No. So next subject."

"This ain't over. Don't you dare think that this is over because it isn't. We are going to talk about this later." I knew I wasn't going to make it to tomorrow without giving her the blow by blow but first I had my own questions.

"Bitch, where were you this morning?"

"Huh?" Lola said looking like a deer in headlights. She doesn't want to answer the question any more than I want to repeat it.

"Huh?" I mocked. "You heard me. Where were you?"

"Oh girl I was just late". That much was obvious. I wasn't about to let her off that easy. Not after she just hounded me.

"Yeah I gather. Why were you late?"

"Huh?"

"Lola. What's up? What are you hiding? And why are you hiding it from me?"

"Nothing girl. I was just running late." She was lying to me and I knew she was, but I wasn't going to press the issue.

"Alright" I said ready to drop it. "You want to come to the mall with me after school? We can finish this then.

"I can't I'm grounded."

"Why?"

"No reason."

"Lola. You're about to make me mad. Stop lying to me. Since when are you grounded? What is going on?" I demanded.
She looked at me and sighed.

"Ok, so my dad dropped me off at school this morning." She stopped. She didn't start again.

"Ok, so what? That happens every day. Your dad dropped you off this morning and?"

"Well, I didn't tell you this, but I had plans to spend the day with Chris."

"Ok what does that have to do with anything?" I asked unsure and curious of what Chris had anything to do with the story.

"After my dad dropped me off, I came in and walked out of the side door of the cafeteria. You know, that door leads to the corner?"

"Yeah" I nod my head

"Well, he turns at to go to work and he saw me as soon as I came out of the door."

"HA" I quickly covered my mouth before anyone could see where it came from. I still felt myself beginning to laugh. I tried to hold it in, but that was short lived. I bust out laughing. I couldn't help it. I laughed uncontrollably for a solid 45 seconds. I know. That was so disrespectful. But still. It was so funny.

"Oh my goodness Lorde! BITCH REALLY?!?"

"I'm sorry I'm sorry. I'm done. I'm done. I'm done" I say calming down.

"Anyway", she rolled her eyes, "he kept driving like he didn't see me, so I kept walking to the bus stop.

"The bus stop?" I can't help but interrupt. "What were you doing at the bus stop? I thought you said you were spending the day with Chris. Why didn't he come get you?" She frowned.

"Shut up and listen Lorde". I motioned for her to continue.

"So, I got to the bus stop and I sat on the bench and my dad comes up and sits beside me." I can't help it. I snicker a little. Lola gives me a serious look and I attempt to hold in my laughs.

"He asked me where I was going and what my plans were" she continued, "I told him the truth. He asked me exactly what you just asked me. Where is he and why he didn't come get me? I already got a lesson from my dad. I don't need one from you too. Needless to say, that's why I'm grounded". I act like I'm letting what she says sink in when really, I'm just giving her a moment before I tell her about herself.

"You may not *need* the lecture, but you're getting one anyway chick. First of all, you know better than to skip school without telling me the details first. How else am I supposed to cover for you and know that you're ok? You're better than that. Secondly, the bus? Really? Girl you don't even catch the bus to school. We don't catch busses for no one. Especially not a boy. Especially not a boy with a car. He is more than capable of coming to get you and returning you back. The bus! You're better than that!" I can see in her face that she's just about had enough. I don't care.

"The bus?" I say before she finally stops me

"Ok Lorde enough. I've let you scold me enough. I get it. I'm better than that and I'll do better. Now, back to you and your lovely morning with Mike Sinclair. I told you about my morning so it's your turn. Are you ready to tell me about that?"

"You know you're going to hear it from somebody anyway."

"Yeah, several times and probably several different versions too. I want to hear it from you. Everybody else can think what they want but I want the true story."
I thought about it for a second.

"Well, I did just laugh at you", I say.

"And scolded me" she added.
She had me there. I had to tell her.

Chapter 2

I woke up to a good morning text from an unknown number. I ignore it. Mike didn't call. I gave him my number and he did not call. I am not happy about this at all. My phone rings. It's Lola calling like she does every morning.

"Hey girl. I'm just making sure you're up and getting yourself together."

"Yeah, I'm up."

"Good because I'm trying to figure out what to t wear today. What you wearin'?"

"Jeans and a t-shirt."

"Jeans and a t-shirt? You always say you're wearing jeans and a t- shirt and then come to school looking runway ready."

"If you call jeans and a t-shirt runway ready then fine. Think about it. I really do wear jeans and a t- shirt every day."

"Ok technically yes, you're right" she said after a moment of thought. But you make it sound so simple. You never describe what you're wearing. You just say *jeans and and a t-shirt* like there's no other way to describe it" she chuckled.

"Look girl, it is supposed to be a little chilly today. Wear your leather pants and that cute orange off the shoulder sweater I got you."

"You know I can't wear that to school".

"Yes, you can just put a tank top on underneath."

"You're a life saver. So, what will your outfit look like?"

"Girl I can barely describe yours to tell you what to wear. Like I said, jeans and a t-shirt. I can't help but laugh. I end the phone call and get ready for school.

On the way to school the thought of Mike not calling crept up on me. I can't believe he didn't call. *Ok, I see how it is. He tracked me down to get my phone number and doesn't use it? How dare he. Never had a boy asked me for my phone number and not use it. Am I being played? Nah, that can't be it. Whatever. When I see him I'm just going to walk by like I don't know him. That'll get his attention.* Mind racing, I didn't even notice him walking right beside me. Success. Accidental, but success, nonetheless.

"Hey Goddess, you just gon' walk right past me?" Mike asked, his voice getting a little pitchy.

"Oh, my bad", I look at him as if I didn't know he had fallen into step, "What's up with you?" I ask nonchalantly and stopping in the middle of the hall, causing a student traffic jam.

"Nothing much" he says, arms outstretched for a hug. I don't move. I just stare at him with raised eyebrows. "What? No hug?" I roll my eyes and oblige but turn and give him a side hug. I pat him on the back like I don't really want to hug him. I did. I just didn't want him to know that I did. He scooped me up and cradled me like a baby.

"Don't give me the side hug. I'm better than a side hug." I cocked my head to the side

"But are you?" I ask with a wrinkled forehead "Are you really better than a side hug?" I cock my head to the side. He looked at me as though I'd given him a riddle he couldn't solve.

"Well, I have to get to class" I said patting his chest; he hadn't put me down yet. He kissed my forehead and

smiled, and I jumped down from his arms to the ground.
"Alright then I'll see you later". I gave a small wave
goodbye and turned and walked away. I could feel his eyes
glued to my butt, but I didn't turn around. I just kept
walking.

"Hey girl, how'd it go last night?" Lola greeted me
as she fell in step. She was really asking if Mike called and
what we talked about. "You know Mike is back there
looking at your booty, right?" I didn't answer either
question. I heard her but my mind was wandering. "What's
up girl?" she said stopping me mid-step and turning me by
the arms to face her.

"Mike didn't call last night" I shrugged "I gave him
my number and he didn't call. This has never happened to
me so I don't know how to feel". I grabbed her arm,
connected it in mine and we began walking again.

"Well," Lola said, "he's still in your face today.
You don't ever see him in a girl face like that. He likes you
girl" I thought about it for a second.

"Probably, but not what you think".

"I'm thinking a relationship maybe. He obviously
want to be your man."

"I figured that. That's why I said probably not what
you think. I mean it sounds good but no. He seems to be
interested, but in what? He didn't call."

"You wanna know what I would do?" Lola had a
sly look on her face.

"No, not really, I got this" I say shaking my head
no, "I'm already doing it my way. I'll let you know how it
goes though." Before she could say anything else, the bell
rang.

"Oh goodness we're late" I say. We quicken our
pace and make it into class just before the teacher closed
the door.

I could not concentrate at all during class. I just kept thinking about Mike not calling me. *Why am I even worried about him calling me? Why am I giving it this much thought? It's not like I like him like that anyway. I mean he not even that cute. I wasn't even thinking about him before yesterday.* The teacher must have told us to pair up because Lola's and my desks were now touching, she seemed to be talking in my direction.

"I'm sorry what did you say?" I said, attempting to dismiss my thoughts.

"I said stop trippin' over that boy. It's only been a day and you know that nobody calls as soon as they get the number. It makes them look weak. Give it a few days and then be mad". I'm not trying to hear anything she's saying. I feel differently than she does, so I try to change the subject.

"Wow" I said, "you just said all of that in one breath. That's talent."

"Did you hear anything I just said?" she asked folding her hands on the desk. I didn't hear one word of what she said because I stopped paying attention, but I'm not about to tell her that.

"Yeah, I heard you. You've got talent kid" I wink at her and smile

"You're a jerk" she rolled her eyes.

"I know. You are too" I shrug.

"Me?" Lola looks surprised

"Yes you. I told you I did not want your advice and look at you. You just can't help yourself" I shrug. Jerk."

"I'm just being a good friend to your ungrateful butt. You are the one over here looking like somebody stole your bike. What's up with you girl? I didn't even think you liked him like that."

"That's the thing, I don't like him like that" I roll my eyes.

"You're lying. You want him."

"No, I don't. I like someone else" I reveal. I can tell she don't believe me because she disregards what I said.

"Girl you a trip. Let's get this work done" she said taking my paper and copying the answers.

I am not lying. I really am into someone else. And just like that I'm not even thinking about Mike. His name is Demitri Braxton. I met him in Georgia over the summer. I was there visiting my aunt for a few weeks. I met him my first day there and the first words from his mouth were

"Wow. I've never seen anyone so beautiful." I was flattered and didn't know what to say so I just gave him my phone number. Demitri Braxton is so handsome, so adorable so…damn why am I only here for two weeks? He has long curly black hair that he lets hang free. He has captivating hazel eyes that lock you in and a stare that force out all your truths.   The next day he sent me a good morning text. It gave me butterflies. It was the first time I had ever gotten one from a boy. Remembering how fine he was didn't hurt. I was even more flattered when I got one that said good night. I answered sweet dreams with a winking emoji and felt smooth. From there he hung around as much as he could without wearing out his welcome.

Before I left my aunt decided to have a big cookout. When it was over Demitri stayed and helped with the cleanup. After helping me with the dishes, *why are teenagers always the ones stuck doing the dishes?* Anyway, after helping me with the dishes we migrate to the living room where everyone else was trying but failing to watch a movie without falling asleep. We found a spot on the floor and sat down. My aunt keeps her house freezing cold, so I pulled a throw blanket from the back of the couch for us to cover up with. Everyone asleep, we start to talk, keeping our voices as low as possible. I lay my head on his chest and I can feel him vibrate when he speaks. Talking turned into kissing and before I knew it his hands were up my skirt. I let out a small moan and my eyes shoot open and look around to make sure no one was awake or heard me. I slowly slide his hands back down my thighs and stand up. His hands still in mine he stands too. We move down the hall where we're sure no one can see, and the kissing commences. After a while he stops and asks about my virginity. I confess that it's still intact. I was afraid of how he would react to my confession, but he didn't trip. At least he didn't seem to be. He started kissing me again. He picked me up and I wrapped my legs around his waist. He carried me into one of the bedrooms and lay me on the bed. He then turns the light on and the television. He sits on the edge of the bed and begin channel surfing. After landing on a movie, he climbs into bed behind me and hold me until we both fall asleep. Before I left the next morning we promised to keep in contact. I didn't know that he'd end up moving here and going to the same high school as me. It was a surprise to see him at my school and an even bigger surprise when I realized that we have every class together. What are the odds? I never told Lola about him because well let's face it the girl has a big mouth and even bigger opinions, and I didn't want to hear either. I haven't really spoken to Demitri since school started so I don't know if he likes me or if what we had should stay where it is.

~ ~ ~ ~ ~

"Damn Goddess again? That's the second time today". I run into Mike on the way to my next class. Literally. I bumped into him and dropped my books. He picked them up but didn't give them back to me.

"Michael" I said in my fake surprised voice.

"It's Mike" he frowned. "Not Michael. Mike"

"Sorry I never heard of a Mike getting mad at being called Michael before" I give a questioning look.

"My mother didn't name me Michael. She named me Mike", he shrugged.

"Oh, my bad. I didn't mean any harm" I apologized.

"No harm done" he smiled and lightened the mood. "So why you keep acting like you don't see me?"

"Oh, I'm not acting. I never run into you this many times in a day. You trying to be seen or something like that?" I say, smiling flirtatiously.

"Something like that", he smiled back. I noticed his dimples before but I had never noticed his smile. He has a wonderful smile. Yes, I said wonderful.

"Well, now that you're seen, what's up?" I say still smiling.

"Ditch class with me."

"Boy please, I said, my smile faded with the quickness, "I'm not ditching class with you. I don't know you like that." I snatch my books from him.

"Know me like what? Girl come on.

"And do what? I ask with a frown.

"So we can talk."

"Talk? Didn't I give you my number?

"Yeah, but I just want to talk to you", he says putting his arm around me.

"Again, didn't I give you my number?" I say slipping out from under his arm. "If you want to see me or talk to me, you can call me", I said looking him straight in the eye. "Set something up. You have my number." I walked away to class just as the bell rang. "Dammit" I said turning around to see him still standing there, "you made me late", I said turning around and continuing to class.

Yeah, he definitely has to call me if he thinks I am considering anything other than a walk to class with him. I'm not about to play myself like that. I'm not like those girls who are just hypnotized by him.

When I got out of class Mike was outside the door waiting for me to come out.

"Mike. You again. I tried to sound bored. "Do you ever go to class? How are you here right now?"

"Mostly always" he shrugged, "I just wanted to come check you real quick" he said.

"Mostly always? I ask with a slight chuckle. What you checkin' me for?

"Not much, just came to check you. See if you wanted to take me up on that offer."

"Offer?" I was confused

"Yeah".

"An offer to ditch class with you? You call that an offer?

"Come on, just roam the halls with me".

"Wait a minute. You want to ditch class and stay in school?"

"Precisely." He nodded his head and rocked back and forth.

"So, just to clarify, your offer is to ditch class with you to roam the halls of the school that holds the classes in which we're ditching to talk after I gave you my number yesterday and you didn't call?" I ask. He doesn't say anything. He just stares at me. It is a stare that claims complete ignorance. Then he sighs and shrugs

"Yeah", he said.

"Mike", I sighed "we just talked about this. Call me when you're ready to talk to me". I walked away. *I just can't believe how stupid boys are* I said to myself as I walked down the hall to my last class.

~ ~ ~ ~ ~

"Girl, you got him" Lola squealed over the phone. She had noticed seeing Mike around more than usual today.

"Girl I don't have shit. He still hasn't called"

"Yeah, but he's checkin' for you every chance he gets."

"Now that I hear it back it sounds kinda stalker-ish"

"Girl shut up. My grand momma said this how boys used to do it in the old days. Calling for them meant that someone was there to see them. Not calling on the phone. So basically, he keep calling and you keep hanging up on the poor boy"

"So you're saying that I have been hanging up on him all day?" She sounds ridiculous but I go along with it anyway.

"Yes ma'am you have been ignoring your gentleman caller all day" she says in her fake southern accent.

"Yeah, but today we call people on the phone when we start getting to know one another, not skip class to roam the halls" I blurt out.

"Skip class to roam the halls?" I could hear the disgust in her voice. "You didn't say that. What kind of stuff is he on? Who does that? Where they do that at?" she said all in one breath. I waited to see if she would continue. "Hello"? she sings dragging out her o.

"Yeah, I'm here. I'm just thinking about it all." I say with a sigh. I consider telling her about Demitri but I decide against it. She wasn't trying to hear it before, so I'll let her keep going on about Mike.

"Well like I said if you want him, you already got him girl so don't even worry about that. I got homework to finish though so I'll see you tomorrow."

"Yeah, me too girl. I'll holla."

As soon as I hung up the phone with Lola my phone rang again. It wasn't Mike. I didn't answer. My phone rang all night long. It was from an unknown caller. I ignored it all night long. I couldn't get what Lola said out of my mind. She seemed to think that I had Mike right where I wanted him. Where I wanted him to be was on the other side of the phone and that is not where he was.

My thoughts turn back to Demitri. We've been in school for over a month now and he hasn't even acknowledged me. Well, if he won't say something I guess I will have to say something. I pick up the phone and call him. As soon as the phone starts ringing, I get nervous and wonder to myself why I didn't just send him a text message.

"Hello" he answers. Butterflies fill my stomach. *Why on earth would I do such a thing?* I want to hang up, but it's too late. I have to say something.

"Hey stranger" I try to sound cool. "I guess I can't say long time no see, so long time no speak." *Why did I just say that? That was so lame.* I was happy when he agreed and continued with the conversation. He said he was glad I finally called. He explained that when he moved here, he got a new phone and lost all of his contacts. We talked for hours. We reminisced about our short time together over the summer and from there the conversation went on and on. We finally got off the phone to take a nap before school.

Chapter 3

As I turned off my alarm this morning, a text came through. I am hoping it is Demitri. We have been talking a lot for the last month and every night we've been falling asleep on the phone. We aren't dating but we do like each other. I check the message and it's him.

Good morning. I know that we talked all night, but when I opened my eyes you were the first thing on my mind.

I smile and I text back and get out off the bed. Another text comes through. It's not Demitri.

Good morning Goddess. Meet me in the auditorium before class

It's Mike. I am not too excited. I mean it was just a text. It has been over a month since I gave Mike my phone number and he still hasn't called. I guess he thinks he doesn't have to. I don't know why he would think that because I told him what was up. I let him know that I was feeling Demetri and that he has major competition. Really Mike is no competition for Demetri, but whatever. I consider not responding. Instead, I reply

Good to know you haven't lost my number

"I don't know why he don't know how to follow simple instructions" I say throwing the phone to the bed and bucking at it before walking away from it to get myself together for school. As I got myself together my phone rang again but I didn't answer it. When I'm done, I check to see who it is, but the caller id said UNKNOWN CALLER.

When I arrived at school, I had no intentions on meeting Mike in the auditorium. I went straight to class. I didn't even stop by my locker first.

"Hey girl, why is everyone crowding the auditorium right now?" Lola greeted me, taking her seat next to me. At the same time Demitri walked in. He didn't say anything he just looked at me. He walked by and winked at me on the way to his seat. I wink back and smile a little without Lola noticing. This has been going on for a while and she still hasn't noticed. I still haven't told her about him yet. I don't know that I will.

"Crowding the auditorium? Are you kidding me?" I say with a wrinkled forehead.

"Nah girl, what's up?"

He must think he's messing with a young girl. He can't mold me. He can't just tell me to be somewhere and I just show up I thought.

"Mike sent me a text this morning telling me to meet him in there. I'm glad I didn't go."

"Why you ain't go?" Lola squealed. She was really on top of my situation with Mike.

"For what? He hasn't even called me yet. I'm not honoring his requests. That takes way more than a good morning text with a request attached. I don't know what y'all think this is. On top of that everybody is there which means he probably told everybody the same thing."

"You might be reading too much into all of this. I don't think it's that serious You know what's really impressive though?" Lola asked.

"What?"

"You said all of that in one breath better than I ever could". We both laughed.

"You might be right", I shrugged, "maybe I am reading too much into it, but oh well if I am. I got this"

"I know you got this girl." I jump, surprised by the vibration of my phone. It was a text. I knew it was Mike, so I looked at it

Hey what's up with the no show?

I chuckled and put my phone down without responding. I could tell Lola was dying to say something, but she held it in. My phone rang. It was Mike. Lola saw it and gasped and looked at me.

"Hello" I answered. I knew I could get him to call. It may be during school hours and it may have taken a month, but he called. I looked at Lola with a look that said *I told you so*.

"Good morning. How are you today? Mike asked

"I'm well thank you" I replied.

"What happened to you this morning? You left me hanging."

"No, I didn't. I never told you I was meeting you" I said with a small chuckle.

"You led me to believe you would though"

"No, I didn't. I said it was nice to see you didn't lose my number, which by the way it is nice to see" I said flirtatiously.

"Well, the bell is about to ring so I have to go" he said, a hint of irritation in his voice.

"Alright, later".

"See, I told you" Lola said as soon as I ended the call. "I told you he was yours if you wanted him. I've been saying it this whole time." She had a big smile of her face that showed all of her beautiful white teeth

"Yes, Lola you did say that. Unfortunately for him this phone call didn't count" I shrugged. Lola's smile faded and she gave me a questioning look.

"He just wanted an immediate response. You heard the call. It didn't count". Lola sat staring at me looking surprised. I laughed at her facial expression and said "I told you I had this".

"You wanted him to call, he called, and you say it doesn't count. I'm starting to think you don't have this." Lola threw her hands up in defeat.

"Really? Think about it girl. Now I know his fingers aren't broken. He already slipped up this time. He'll call again. Next time it'll be on purpose with purpose."

"Yeah ok girl. You sure about that?" she asked looking skeptical.

"Absolutely not"

"And you're sure you not tryna make him your man?"

"Yeah girl I'm sure" I say trying to sound reassuring. The truth is at this point I don't really know what I want out of Mike. I haven't had the chance to get to know him well enough to know. We keep playing this stupid game where he shows up outside of my classroom to try to get me to skip class and I reiterate how I gave him my number and suggest he use it. It's honestly starting to bore me.

"Nah I think he about to be your man. Otherwise, why are you playing games with that boy?"

"Oh no no no he is Not! He ain't ready for a real girlfriend. He can't even wrap his mind around calling. It's been over a month and you think I'm supposed jump for him because he made a brief phone call? Are you dating someone who hasn't picked up the phone to call you?"

"No", she shakes her head and shrug.

"Exactly" I say with an aggressive nod. "Anyway, I don't want him as a boyfriend. I told you. I'm into someone else. This is something different. I'm not playing games with him. I just want him to call me on purpose. I can't rock with him if he doesn't." I said finally taking a much needed breath.

"What do you mean you can't rock with him? I thought you said you don't want him to uh...never mind."

"What? Tell me"

"Well first of all you didn't answer my question. Secondly, this "something different" you're referring to sounds like he's your man." She is right and I know it. I don't want him to be my man, but the more I talk the more I realize that I've been giving her reason to believe otherwise. I still haven't told her about Demitri. I keep trying to give her a hints to ask about this "someone else" but either she don't notice or don't care. I'm thinking I should just come out and tell her about him. No. That's not a good idea.

"Girl, it's cool" Lola said interrupting my thoughts. I know you got this." She put her hand on my shoulder and gave it a squeeze. She turned around and I tried to pay attention to what the teacher was saying.

When class was over, I was low key looking for Mike to be there. When he wasn't, I was a little relieved but slightly disappointed. As I walked to my next class out of nowhere, I was blinded from behind by someone's hands.

"Guess who?" he whispered in my ear. I could smell that familiar, intoxicating scent. I reached up and I could feel those rock-hard arms. There was no need to guess. I knew exactly who it was. I was excited to see him, but I wasn't about to let him see it.

"Let's see" I said as I took each hand down from my eyes and wrapped his arms around my shoulders. I lean back and whisper "Mike". He didn't move he just whispered back

"Walk with me".I hesitate for a second and whisper back

"No".

"No?" he said, breaking the silence.

"No Mike" I sigh and turn and face him "the next step to getting to know me is to call me."

"Alright" he said, "you want me to call you here you go". He picked up his phone and called me right then and there. Just as I was about to answer the phone, I hear

"Miss Alexander do not answer that phone in my school if it is not your mother." It was the principal.

"Really Mrs. Monroe? Why you hatin'?" I asked her with a smile

"I said put it away Miss Alexander don't make me say it again" she raised her eyebrows. "It'll be mine" she said. I decline the call and put my phone away.

"That's messed up Mrs. Monroe, you ain't say nothing to Mr. Sinclair right here", I yelled behind her as she walked away.

"Nice try, but it wouldn't have counted anyway" I shrug, "Walk me to class?"

"I can do that" he took my arm and asked, "So this call wouldn't have worked. Does that mean this morning's call didn't count?"

"That's exactly what it means. You weren't trying to get to know me this morning. You only called because you felt some kind of way about me not meeting you in the auditorium."

"Why didn't you come?"

"You must be used to people just doing whatever you tell them to do huh? I'm sorry, but I'm not the one."

"I just wanted to show you something"

"Seems to me that you had a big enough audience this morning."

"That wasn't my fault. I don't know why they were there."

"Yeah ok. So, what did you want to show me?"

"It's cool. You had to be there. Good thing I had a big enough audience, though right?" He looked over at me and smiled.

"Cute. Real cute" I said nodding my head.

"You seem to think so".

"Not really."

"Huh?"

"I have to get to class. Call me". I rush into the classroom before he could say anything else.

As I take my seat right before the bell rings I start to regret not meeting Mike this morning. My regret doesn't last long. If he really wanted to show me something and didn't invite the rest of his audience then it wouldn't have been a 'you-had-to-be-there' thing. He would have shown me what was for me.

I looked over to say something to Lola and I realize that she isn't there. Instead I got caught in Demetri's gaze. He winked at me. I gave a slight smile and turn away twirling my hair as to not be detected by anyone else. I noticed again that Lola wasn't in class yet and wondered where she was. Just as I was about to ask someone she walks in and hurries to her seat. She's wearing sunglasses but I can tell that she's been crying by the color of her nose.

"You're Late Miss Bordeaux. Where is your note? And please remove your sunglasses"

"I don't have one. I know it's unexcused. Sorry." Lola said irritated, snatching the shades from her face and plopping down into her seat.

"Lola, what's wrong?" I whisper. She looked at me as though contemplating on whether or not to tell me.

"Lola you've been crying. Why were you crying?" I try not to sound demanding, but I couldn't help it. I was concerned for my friend.

"Ladies you can talk about whatever you want on your own time. Right now, is my time" the teacher said before she could answer me. I guess I'd have to wait until class was over to find out what was wrong. And it couldn't go by fast enough.

~ ~ ~ ~ ~

We barely get out of class before I start questioning Lola.

"Ok girl what is wrong with you? Why are you crying?" I pull Lola into the bathroom and notice she is still a little upset.

"It's Chris" she sighed "I saw him on the way to class and he wanted me to leave school with him."

"Girl no, we have a test next period."

"I know. That's what I told him. He tried to get me to make it up.

"How Lola? Your mom coming up here to say you missed class to be with your boyfriend? With your luck they'll call your mother before you get home."

"I know Lorde. I'm here. I didn't go. I told him I wasn't going with him and he broke up with me."

"He broke up with you?" I was confused "Why did he break up with you?

"Yeah. Talking about I don't love him enough. I told him I only love him a couple of months' worth of love because that's how long I've known him. Not enough to fail for him though. Who is in love this early anyway?"

My head was spinning. Having a boyfriend is supposed to be fun. Lola doesn't look like she's been having fun at all. Love? After a few weeks? Here I am stressing about two boys when in reality I really don't want a boyfriend if this is what having one means.

"On top of that you just got in trouble for trying to skip school for him and he didn't even have the decency to come and get you or to check on you when you got caught" I said. "Who does he think he is?"

"Yeah" she continues, "and he told me to catch the next bus. Do you know he had the nerve to get mad when I didn't show up?" Lola shook her head in disgust. I don't want the kind of drama she has. I don't see how she wants to deal with this kind of mess.

"Ok so why were you crying? Sounds to me like you're finally rid of that asshole."

"Yeah, I guess you're right. I really liked him though. But what's up with you and Mike?" Lola asked attempting to take the spotlight off herself and onto me. She spoke in past tense so that I would believe her. I don't believe her. She still likes that boy, and she is not going to stop dealing with him. I already know it, but I don't say anything. I just let her change the subject.

"I see he's not mad at you. Still in your face and thangs." We both giggled.

"Nah he's not mad at me. He just doesn't like to do things any other way but his own."

"You're the same way. You might as well give in to that boy. You know you like him. Maybe if you do things his way he'll reciprocate."

I had to admit that Lola made a little bit of sense. Maybe I should try things a little different. Use other methods to get what I want. The problem is that I don't really know what I want from him. Also, I've already made progress doing things the way I've been doing them and taking dating advice from Lola right now didn't seem like the smart thing to do.

"Well," I shrug, "yeah I think...I think I got this." Even I'm not convinced by the words coming out of my mouth. We both knew I was not saying what I was thinking. A few girls came into the bathroom and stood in front of the mirrors. I looked at Lola. She locked her arm into mine and we left.

Chapter 4

When I got home there was a guy on my porch. I knew right away it wasn't Mike. He was too tall to be Mike. As I walked up to my porch I asked.

"May I help you?" He was also way too cute to be Mike. He blocked me from the last step.

"Yes. You could stop ignoring my calls and text messages" he smiled.

"Ignoring your calls?" I was genuinely confused, but then I remembered all of the calls I ignored from that unknown caller when I wanted Mike to be the one calling.

"Do I know you?"

"Yeah, you better princess. I've been calling you to tell you I was coming home. Now I am home." As soon as he called me princess I knew exactly who was standing in front of me.

"Oh my goodness TREY!" I squealed, dropping my backpack and throwing my hands around his waist. "I missed you so much." I let him go and backed up. "I didn't even recognize you."

"I figured you wouldn't. I changed a lot over the last 2 years. I got taller," he smiled.

"Tell me about it" I say looking him up and down admiring his newfound fineness.

"All of that fineness wasted on you" I shake my head.

Before he was sent to boarding school Trey had a low cut fresh haircut. He was really short not having had a growth spurt yet and he was developing acne. Now he's six feet tall, has long dark brown locs and no acne. Just the same beautiful dark skin that seemed to sparkle in any lighting. He has always been stylish and that hasn't changed either.

"You don't exactly look the same either. Good thing you changed before high school" He smiled.

"I don't know what you're talking about. I've always been this pretty" I flip my hair. I know I am lying. I had a bad bout with acne in middle school. I'm so glad he wasn't here to witness it. I'm even happier that it cleared up before high school.

"Slow down there princess you're not that pretty now" he said laughing.

"Shut up" I punch him in the arm.

"Oh, my goodness I am so excited you're back!" I squeal. "The rest of this year is about to be bananas."

"Tell me about it. I start school tomorrow. Who's going to be the first to get jealous of you walking around with the new boy?"

"Probably Mike" I say but before I think to explain who he is I think of Lola. "Oh my goodness I have to call Lola. She's going to be so hype."

"Lola? No she isn't. We don't even like each other". He looked disgusted at the sound of her name.

"Yeah, but I don't listen to her and now that you're back she has help with little ol' me. She's going to be happy."

"Yeah, you always have been a piece of work".

"Shut up boy" I punch him in the arm.

Trey Briarwood is my best friend. Yeah, Lola can be considered my best friend but not like Trey. Trey is my absolute best friend forever and ever amen. He has been my best friend since birth. No exaggeration. Our parents have been best friends since high school. They even started their medical practice together. When we were eleven, I was grounded for getting suspended from school. I decided to pay my parents back by running away. I convinced Trey to come with me. We caught a bus to the Greyhound bus station and purchased two tickets to New York. We got caught and Trey got shipped off to boarding school for two years. That was the last time I seen or heard from him. Our parents decided they were tired of us always getting into trouble together, so it was their way of separating us. It was not the worst two years of our lives, but it was definitely the dullest.

We catch up on the goings on of the last two years. He tells me all about boarding school and I catch him up on what's been going on at school and with my life.

When I show up this morning with Trey on my arm Lola approaches us instantly.

"So this is why you didn't show up after school yesterday? We had plans remember?" she frowns at Trey as we approach.

"Well hello to you too" I say noticing Lola's frown isn't real. She is actually flirting with Trey a little. She has no idea who he is otherwise she would not be flirting. He doesn't respond the way she wants him to.

"Hey lil Lola. Surprised Lorde is still your friend" he rubs the top of her head. In that instance she knew exactly who she was looking at.

"Trey? Damn man I thought you was somebody real. It's just you. I almost forgot that I hate you boy".

"I could never forget that I hate you. Just stay out of my face. I don't want people to think I like you." He looked around as if he's making sure no one is looking in his direction.

"Yes" I step in between them "this is the reason I didn't show up yesterday. You can't be too upset though because you definitely didn't call. You must have been unavailable. What were you up to missy?

"I don't want to be a part of this conversation" Trey interrupts. "Point me in the direction of the office please."

"Girl just take him. I'll talk to you about it later".

~ ~ ~ ~ ~

I'm standing at the front desk with Trey, and someone blinds me from behind.

"Guess who". I pull his hands down and turn around to face Mike. I look over to Trey and back to him.

"Hey Mike. Why aren't you in class?"

"I was on my way there and I got a little distracted when I saw you, Goddess" he flashed a smile.

"You're pretty easily distracted, I'm learning." I sneak a peek at Trey. He is leaning over the counter with his mouth in his palm trying to mask the fact that he is trying not to smile. He does not make eye contact. I look back to Mike. "It's cool. I tend to have that effect on people." I nod my head. We talk for a few minutes before he notices the boy standing next to me.

"New guy" he nods at Trey.

"Yeah hey" Trey steps in between us and extends his hand for a handshake. "I'm Trey. Trey Briarwood".

"Mike Sinclaire" he says shaking Trey's hand.

"Alright Lorde, you ready to show me around"? He turns from Mike and faces me. He makes kissy faces, and I try to ignore him.

"Yeah, let's go" I move Trey to the side. "Mike I'll see you later" I say avoiding eye contact with Trey.

I consider telling Mike that Trey is not only a new student in school, but he's also my best friend. I decide against it. I'll let him wonder who he is. It's only healthy.

"You will absolutely see me later." He says flirtatiously. I turn and hurry out of the office.

"So that's Mike. You like dude?" I think for a moment.

"No, were just becoming friends"

"If he said that he just wants to be friends with you he's lying."

"Why do you say that?"

"For one he calls you goddess"

"So what? You call me princess."

"Yeah but I've been calling you that since we were five and I didn't know the difference between being a lord and you name being Lorde." He chuckles. I wasn't trying to impress you. I was trying to make sense of life." He shrugs. I remind him that Mike has my number and hasn't called me or asked me out. I then shift the conversation to all of the eyes that's been on him already. As we continue our conversation, I show Trey around the school and to his classes and leave him where he's supposed to be.

~ ~ ~ ~ ~

During my lunch period Mike found me and requested yet again that I walk with him. I hesitated for a second then heard myself saying

"Alright then let's roam." I turn around and we just stood there. Standing about six feet apart we just stared for a moment.

"I like you Goddess". He said and he sounded sincere.

"You don't know me", I say nonchalantly.

"I want to know you though. That's why we're walking."

"No, that's why you should have called me." I roll my eyes, "And we are not walking. We are standing in the middle of the hallway." He stepped over and turned me to face him and looked at me for a second then he smiled. He dropped his hands from my shoulders and took my hand and we began to walk. We walked around the whole school. It was much bigger than I thought.

"So, what made you give me your number?" He stopped to put me on his back.

"Curiosity," I said as I jumped up. "What made you not use it?"

"Cute, kid. What are you so curious about?"

"I'm not a kid. And you. I hear the girls tell stories about you and they make it seem like you have a penis made of gold or something?"

"Did you just say penis?" He stopped walking.

"Yes, I did".

"Who the hell says penis?" he asked shrugging his shoulders.

"Well, that's what it's called" I said giving a confused look. "What do you call it?"

"Oh, I see" he raised a finger and began to shake it. "You're one of those smart ones."

"What's one of those smart one's?" I asked not knowing if I should be offended or not.

"You're the freaky genius type" he said continuing to walk .

"Well, I wouldn't say all of that. I like to think of myself as a genius but" I buried my face into his back, "I'm a virgin".

He laughed "Really? And you chose me to lose your virginity to out of pure curiosity?"

"Arrogant much?" I asked, raising both my head and my eyebrows.

"What you mean?" He was genuinely confused.

"Lose my virginity to you?" I jumped down from his back. "Who said anything about having sex with you?" I said putting my hands on my hips.

"Then what are we talking about?" He asked shrugging his shoulders. I couldn't believe he didn't understand. I thought I made it clear. I guess not.

"Oh goodness, you stupid boy" I say rolling my eyes. "It's not that deep. I just want to see it", I shrug.

"You just want to see it? He frowns. Why didn't you just ask?" he says as if it would be that easy to just ask.

"I didn't know you were that open and...Well we're not there yet. Or at least I didn't think we were."

"Oh we're there little lady. You just told me you're a virgin which means I'm not touching you. We can be friends though."

"All boys want virgins. It's not that you're not touching me, it's that I'm not touching you. You're right though. We can be friends. Now let me see it".

"No way", he was skeptical, "seriously?"

He was considering it. I knew I had him right there.

"Yeah, pull it out". I tried to sound reassuring. He looked around and opened the door to an empty dark classroom. We went in and I turned on the lights. "No keep them off, he said". Turning off the lights defeats the purpose but I turned them off anyway. He pulled out his penis and it was huge. He was right to keep the lights off because I would have definitely drawn attention to the empty classroom. I lie to you not it was the size of a cucumber and it wasn't even hard yet. I was fascinated. I reached out to touch it but he moved away.

"What?" I frowned.

"What? Is this the first time you're seeing one?"

"This big, yeah. I've seen and turned down quite a few but....woooow". I reached again but he smacked my hand down. "Just let me touch it" I demanded

"No, friends don't touch friends' genitals" he snapped. I flip the light on.

"They also don't show each other their genitals and here we are so come on" I said reaching out and this time grabbing it before he could move out of the way.

I poked it. Then I rubbed it and it began to grow. The bigger it got, the bigger my eyes got. I looked at him. He stood there smiling. He was proud that he got that reaction from me. Or maybe he was just proud of the size of his penis. I don't know.

"Ok so we gotta do it now" I said swallowing hard.

"Oh no you're not ready for this. You're a virgin", he said slightly frowning his face up.

"Yet your penis got hard", I looked down, "and it still is. I told you, it wasn't that you weren't touching me, but that I wasn't touching you." I glanced at the clock, "Let's get out of here. The bell's about to ring".

I left the room and started to walk. When he finally caught up we walked with no words.

"You are one interesting girl" he said finally breaking the silence. We were now approaching his locker.

"Interesting? Is that good or bad?"

"It's good. It's not what I expected. I like you."

"Well then it's a good thing we're friends now right," I said winking at him and giving a slight smile. The bell rang, "I have to go, I'll see you later", I turned and walked away.

At my locker Trey and Lola are waiting for me.

"Where were you? They asked in unison. They complained that they had to entertain one another at lunch without me. I'm sure they were exaggerating because at least three girls walked by eyeing Trey while he reprimanded me for leaving him with Lola.

"You do know that you don't have to hang together, right? I look from one friend to the other.

Chapter 5

A few days had gone by and I hadn't seen or heard from Mike. I almost forgot about him until my phone rings.

"Hello" I answered my phone. I wasn't in the mood to talk to anyone, but I answered anyway.

"Hey Goddess" It was him. It was Mike. I had already deleted his number. I didn't think he would ever actually call me again. I was caught completely off guard.

"It's Lorde" I finally answer "Lorde suits me perfectly once you get to know me" I say finally getting my wits about myself.

"I look forward to that" he said.

"Ok so I guess that's not what this call is about."

"Oh on the contrary. I'm calling for that very purpose."

"Ok. What's up?" I ask waiting for him to get to his point. He's not that great on the phone.

"I want to show you something, but I don't know if you're about that life." He thinks he has me figured out. I go along with it anyway.

"Yes I am", I said trying to sound tough.

"Ok then meet me tomorrow during lunch in the photography room."

"Alright" I respond. "I'll be there."

"Don't stand me up like you did me in the auditorium last time" he said with a chuckle

"I won't" I said." I'll be there". I wanted to argue that I didn't stand him up before, but I decided against it. I'm glad I didn't because the rest of the conversation went amazing. He turned out to be better on the phone than he originally let on. We talked all night long about absolutely everything. Demitri called a few times while we were on the phone, but I ignored his calls. When we got off the phone, I felt like I had known him forever. Still, I was unsure of what is happening between us. Something is happening and I have to figure out what it is.

~ ~ ~ ~ ~

I decide to really meet Mike in the photography room. I am surprised to see that we are alone. He picks up a camera and start snapping pictures of me. I start striking poses. He came closer to me steadily snapping his camera. When he got to me, he picked me up placed me on the desk placed the camera under my skirt and snapped a picture. I slapped his face.

"First of all, greet me before snapping nudes. Secondly, you can't do that. Someone will see it. My face is in all of those photos. They'll know that that's my vagina."

"Don't freak, its digital ok. I'll just delete the pictures" Mike said rubbing the side of his face. "Or we can develop them right now and then get rid of the film." He said with raised eyebrows still holding his face.

"We can do that?" I asked

"Of course we can. What did you think I wanted to show you?"

"Honestly? Your penis" I shrugged

"Well, there are pictures of that on this roll too so you're in luck" he said and chuckled.

He showed me the process of developing film.

"I thought you said it was digital. You wouldn't have to develop film if the camera was digital." I look at him. He just smiled. While we waited for the pictures to dry, we talked. Ok, I talked, and he listened.

"I wonder why the school doesn't have digital cameras. This is cool, but today is all about instant gratification." He didn't say anything. Just smiled as he listened to me ramble. I decided to see if he was actually listening.

"I think you'd be a good first. You just can't hurt me. Your penis is freakishly large. Just don't hurt me". He shot me a surprised look. Oh yeah, he was listening.

"Ok, wow on the subject change and no. That's impossible. Your hole is probably the size of a pencil tip. I don't want to take your virginity. I am not the guy for that job. Besides, you want your first time to be perfect. Romantic" he said with a look that I wasn't familiar with.

Mike looked serious, like he really meant what he was saying to me, but he also looked…I don't know what the look is. At the moment I don't care. Remembering his rock-hard penis my juices were flowing. I wanted to have him, and I wanted it now. I didn't want to wait. My idea of the perfect first time was with someone who knew what they were doing and that's him.

"You're not going to hurt me because you like me so let's just do it".

Mike moved in closer, picked me up and placed me on the teacher's desk. He released his erect penis from his jean and used it to play with my vagina but he didn't put it in. He did this for two seconds too long. I held his face in my hands and looked him in the eye and said, "It's ok. I want to do this." He still looked a little skeptical, but he didn't break eye contact. He slipped a finger into my vagina and felt the wetness pour from me. He backed away.

"I can't do this to you. I'm not going to do this to you".

"Ok" I said jumping down off of the desk and adjusted my skirt. "Let's go I said turning out the lights as he put his penis away. I turned to open the door but he caught my hand and said "wait". I turned around and he picked me back up and put me back up on the table. He didn't bother turning the lights back on. He lifted my skirt and removed my panties and put them in his pocket. He kissed me nervously and said

"I said I can't do *that* to you".

He opened my legs and kissed each thigh one by one over and over again until my legs were spread wide and he dipped his tongue inside.

"You just came." He lifted his head after a few seconds.

"No I didn't" I said pushing his head back down.

"Yes, you did". He raised his head to look at me again.

"Wouldn't I feel it?" I asked pushing his head back down

"Yeah I guess so" he said, this time staying put.

"Well, then I didn't. I'm just extra wet." I had no idea what I was talking about, but I thought it was impossible for me to have come already.

"If you say so" he shrugged "you taste like peaches" he said and dipped his head back under my skirt. It was like nothing I'd ever felt before. I can't believe this is happening. Suddenly excitement reaches my core and rush through my body faster than I thought it would. I have never felt such an intense feeling. When he was done he slipped my panties back on and adjusted my skirt for me. We stood in place embracing one another for a a good two minutes. We left just in time for it to not get awkward. We made sure to grab our photos and destroy the film and we left without a word. We walked a few steps in awkward silence until finally he broke it.

"So look", he said to me as we walked back to familiar territory, "you have to do me a favor".

"What's that?" I ask, unsure of what he was about to request and bracing myself for the worst.

"You're not ready yet. For sex. I know you think you are, but you're not ready yet", he said with a thoughtful look on his face. "But when you are ready, and I mean really ready, not just bloodthirsty and hormonal, come holla at me. Don't just give it away. Let me show you what's up." I thought for a minute. I was ready and we both knew it but I knew what he meant. My hormones were raging out of control and somehow in the last 10 minutes he'd controlled them. I didn't want him to think he was right.

"You know the real truth is that you aren't ready. My name is Lorde, you dubbed me Goddess, remember that? Now you've just tasted the sweetest nectar the world has to offer, and your world is changed. You can call me when you're really ready for change. You have my number". I kissed him on the cheek. "When you want to be seen, I'll see you around". I walk away. As usual I could feel his eyes glued to my backside. I know he'll be back around.

~ ~ ~ ~ ~

Okay, so, I know I said he'd be back around, but I didn't know he'd be around so soon. When I got home from school, my experience still fresh on my mind, there he was on my front porch, ringing my doorbell.

"No one's home" I said from behind him. He turned around with a smile.

"Goddess" he said. Dammit his smile is gorgeous and contagious. I couldn't hold mine back.

"My name is Lorde" I said still smiling

"Goddess suits you better", he said with a wink, still smiling.

"So what brings you by? And before I get home?"

"Oh, I thought you'd be home already. I can't stop thinking about what you said." My smile faded when I realized what had just happened. Mike just showed up at my house without permission. I didn't even tell him where I lived so how did he know?

"I said you have my number, and you could give me a call, not stop by. How do you even know where I live?"

"I didn't know you lived here until I came by to visit my cousin, Veronica"

"My next-door neighbor, Veronica?" I asked pointing next door.

"Yeah. I noticed your last name on the mailbox and decided to try my luck. I mean how many Alexander families can there be around here?"

"Some luck" I said, my smile returning. So, you couldn't get me off your mind huh? I shift my weight to one side and tilt my head.

"That's not what I said" he shakes his head.

"You sure? Because that's what I heard." I tilt my head to the other side and winked at him.

"All of a sudden I'm not so sure" he said moving in closer to me.

"Well, if you're not so sure then maybe you should have called first." I took a step back.

"I was here, I tried my luck and it worked", he shrugged taking a step forward.

"Ok lucky guy" I say stepping forward, "you found me, now what?" I shrugged

"Now we talk" he said. I look at his mouth. I don't want to talk. I wanted him to do that thing with his tongue again that he did tome earlier. Mike turned around and headed back to my porch and took a seat. I followed and sat next to him and said,

"Alright, let's talk. So why couldn't you stop thinking about me?" I smiled.

"You're a funny girl" he said, "but for real though I can't stop thinking about what you said earlier".

"What did I say earlier?"

"You know, all that about being ready for change" he said with a serious face and soft, thoughtful eyes

"Oh yeah I said call me when you're ready for change. So what? You old-fashioned? Calling means stop by?" I nudge his arm

"I know I know you gave me your number, but I like looking at you when we talk" he said sliding closer to me again.

"We have apps for that" I smirk

"I know but still. I wanted to see you in person. You know I like you right?"

"Yeah, I know. I like you too but I'm not trying to be your girl."

"Look at you, jumping the gun. I didn't ask you that" he said and after a half of a second of thought he asked "Why not? I mean I'm not asking but why not?"

"I can think of two reasons off the top. You don't show any real interest" I hold up one finger "and you don't follow directions very well" I put up the second finger. He didn't look upset. He looked more thoughtful.

"Well, you did say change. And I actually follow directions very well" he winked. "It may not be the way you want it but it's always for the best" he smiled. "I still can't have sex with you though. I can't do that to you."

"No, you can't do that to *you*" I laughed. "And what does sex have anything to do with anything? Did I just agree to something that I don't know about? Who's jumping the gun now?"

I can see why he likes talking face to face. It's different. It's more real than talking on the phone. The connection is different. We sat and talked about "what we are". It is obvious that we are becoming more than friends but we definitely have no intentions on dating. At least not one another.

"So, what is it with you collecting numbers but not calling?" I asked. He shrugged.

"I guess I just don't like the phone."

"So why ask a girl for her phone number?"

"It's just a good icebreaker I guess." He shrugged again.

"Why you trippin'? I called you."

"I'm not trippin'. And we're just friends so that doesn't count."

"Oh it counts. I called you three times before knowing we were going to be just friends. I had full intentions onnn nothing at all" he said catching himself before completing his sentence. I laughed at him. I already knew what he was going to say.

"You think you called me three times. That's laughable" I laughed. "You made a fluke call one day to throw a temper tantrum but go off sir" I joked.

"See what I'm saying Lorde. That's why I call you Goddess" he said rubbing my cheek, "you're really gorgeous but also kind of mean and slightly scary. Just how I imagine a goddess to be", he smiled. We sat on my porch and talked until my mother called me in for dinner and asked if my friend would be staying.

Chapter 6

It's been a week since Mike showed up at my house and I haven't seen or heard from him since. I don't really know what to think at this point so I'm not thinking about it at all. I tried. I thought we were becoming…something, but I guess I was wrong. Maybe he doesn't want to be my friend. I tried to talk to Trey about it but I guess he's decided that he doesn't approve of Mike. I usually respect his opinion but not on this one. Especially considering his active dating condition. Trey Briarwood is the new name around school. He corrects people when they call him Mikes protégé. The very reason he doesn't approve of him for me.

As I walk down the hall, I notice a cute boy standing in the middle of the hall. I don't say anything. I just keep walking.

"Hi" he said with a smile. He must be new because I don't know who he is. I lightly blushed as I walked past him and give a slight smile.

"Lorde Alexander, right?" I stopped in my tracks and turned around on my heels.

"Do I know you?" I'm almost sure I don't know him, but it's possible that I might.

"Not at the moment"

he said approaching me. Something about him was very familiar.

"Do you know me?"

"Not really. No, I don't".

"Okay, soooo how do you know my name?" I squint my eyes and tilt my head.

"I asked around", he shrugged. I guess he couldn't read my face, so he continued. "I'm Brian". Searching my brain to for memories of a Brian and nothing is coming to me.

"Okay Brian, why are asking around about me?"

"I saw you and I wanted to know who you were" he shrugged. "Asking questions is the easiest way to get answers."

"I see. So, what did you find out?"

"Huh?" The look on his face was that of a person who had no idea what he was going to say next.

"What did you find out when you asked around?"

"Whatchu mean?" He asked feigning confusion.

"I know you found out more than my name. So," I shrugged, "tell me."

"Nah", he lied, "I just found out your name." I gave him a look of suspicion and he said, "I don't like to form my opinion based on other people's opinion, so I just got your name. That way I could meet you on my own and form my own opinion." He was not convincing at all. I didn't believe a word of it. He definitely got more than my name.

"Yeah right. It's cool though. I won't press you out. I know you got more than my name though", I said with a smile. "Bye Brian" I said turning on my heels and walking away.

I have to admit that Brian is cute. No not cute he is fine as hell. I mean bayBEEE. he has no business being that good looking. But who is he? I don't know him, so he has to be new. I would remember seeing him around and I certainly have not. Where did he come from? And why is he so damn fine?

"Hey Lola, you know a boy name Brian?"

"Yeah. Brian what?"

"Brian uh I don't know. Dang! I didn't get his last name".

"Well how do you know him?"

"I don't know him, but he knows me." I turn my head up in thought.

"How does he know you?" she frowned

"Apparently he's been asking around about me."

"Is he cute?"

"Girl he is gorgeous." I shook her by the shoulders.

"Damn girl you lucky. Stuff like this never happens to me. Why does interesting stuff always happen to you?" she pouted.

"That's because you're the interesting thing that happens to people." I hug her and then hold her back out at arm's length to look her in the face.

"You my dear are a big ball of interesting."

"And so is this Brian" she smiles. We have to figure out who he is. You say he was asking around about you".

"Yeah", I shrug.

"Ok well no one asked me anything and nobody sent him my way for tea. Sounds a little suspicious."

"I know, strange right. Nobody sends him your way and he know my first and last name."

"Wait first and last?"

"Yeah, that's how he got my attention. He called me by my first and last name."

"Why would someone knowing your first and last name be strange? I mean we are in school." Trey walks up and join the conversation

"You know what?" I laugh, "you're right" I felt silly not thinking about that.

"Oh, girl we have got to figure out who he is. He might be your new bae. Mike is going to be so jealous." Lola chuckles.

"What do *you* get out of Mike being jealous?" Trey asks.

I think it's impossible for Trey to hide his dislike for Lola. He's been telling me since he got back to keep an eye on Lola because she isn't the friend that I think she is.

"No, he's not. Mike and I are just friends." I answer before she can acknowledge what Trey said.

"Yeah, friends who kiss." Both Trey and I give her a confused look then we look at each other and back to her.

"What?" She don't even think she said anything wrong. We look at her for another second. Trey tells me he will talk to me later and walks away in one direction and I go in the other leaving her in place. I know the girl has a big mouth and big opinions. I know she comments on things that she has no real knowledge of and that has absolutely nothing to do with her. I just never thought she would turn it on to me. One minute she's bigging me up for talking to Mike and the next she's encouraging me to go after someone else. I don't know what her agenda is but I have plans of my own. Trey is right. She may not be the friend I think she is. I'll have to keep my eyes open.

~ ~ ~ ~ ~

I didn't see Brian for the rest of the day. I didn't know his last name so I thought it might be weird to even ask around about him. I mean his name is Brian. The name of probably half the boys in school. I'd probably be better off asking around about a boy name John Smith without his last name.

"What's got your hair follicles burning?" Mike asked approaching and putting his arm around my shoulder.

"Huh?"

"She's trying to figure out who some Brian guy is and how he knows her", Lola answered before the question could even registered in my brain.

"Oh, Brian what? I might know him."

"She doesn't know" Lola answered for me again. "She didn't get his last name". She's getting a little too much enjoyment out of this.

"Well how does he know you?" He looks from Lola to me then back to Lola when she answers the question again before I can.

"He's been asking around about her." I could tell that Mike was getting annoyed with Lola, so I gave in and finally said

"Lola I can answer for myself." Trey is right. I'm definitely keeping my eye on Lola. I loop my arm into Mike's and we begin to walk.

"Where have you been?" I ask trying to change the subject.

"Well, no one's attention is harder to get than yours so I'm sure he asked a lot before approaching you", he said disregarding my question. I let it slide.

"Well, that's the thing. He didn't exactly approach me."

"He didn't approach you?" Mike gave me a confused look.

"Nah", I shrugged. "I was walking by him and our eyes met. Just as I was passing, he said my name."

"That's strange. I can check and see if I can get some information if you want."

"It is a nice offer but no thank you. That's not my style."

"What's that supposed to mean?"

"It means that I'm leaving it alone. If he wants to get to know me, he'll figure it out".

I could tell that Mike was a little jealous. Lola was right. He is definitely jealous. He doesn't like something that he was hearing. We haven't spent a lot of time together, so I still don't know what it is or why.

"So, what happened after he confirmed your name?"

"Nothing", I shrugged. "We exchanged a sentence or two and I went to class".

"Dang girl he didn't ask for your number or nothing?" Lola said. We both turned around and shot her a look. I didn't know she was walking with us this whole time.

"My bad. I know how to read the room. I'll see ya'll later." She stopped and put her hand on Mike's shoulder and said,

"You need to stop playing with her if you want her to stop playing with you." After Lola walked away Mike got quiet.

"So" I said.

"So" he said.

"Are you ready to go back to my question now?" He gave a thoughtful look and said

"No. Not particularly. You should get to class." He is definitely upset about something. I'm sure he'll let me know sooner or later. I'm not too worried about it. He still has to answer for his disappearing act.

"I told you to watch out for that girl. She's jealous of you". Trey said pointing at me.

"No, she is not jealous of me. Lola is my best friend". He looked at me like I had three heads.

"She is not your best friend. I am your best friend."

"So is she" I laugh

"So, you told her about Demitri?" He already knows the answer to the question.

"No, I haven't told her yet"

"Ok so you told her we know about your little rendezvous with Mike then". He knows the answer to this question too.

"No" I shake my head "Only you know about that, but that doesn't mean she isn't my b-

"Baby girl, that's exactly what it means" he cut me off. "If she is your best friend, you wouldn't hide it from her. You would tell her everything. That's what you girls do." He's right, she isn't my best friend.

"That's what I have *you* for. I don't tell anyone *everything* except for you."

"That's because I'm your best friend. She is just a damn bobble head." he smiled a smile of satisfaction. Like he just won a prize or something.

"Nah but for real I don't know why you're still friends with her. that girl is going to cause problems for you sooner than later". Trey's phone rang. He looked at it and smiled.

"I see you're not having any problems fitting in." He looked up.

"Oh that's definitely not a problem with me." He smiled and then it faded. "It's still fucked up you left me with the bobble head at lunch on my first day though".

"I didn't leave you with Lola" I laughed. His phone was still ringing. "Will you answer that thing".

Chapter 7

Mike must have really taken what Lola said into consideration about not playing with me. He's been coming around a lot more often to walk me to class. He drives me to school when he can, and he has been making it a point to text me before bed. He still does not call. We hang out from time to time, but Lola is always around, so we don't get too comfortable. It's not really going anywhere beyond friendship, but maybe that's all we should be is friends. I kind of like him, but not that much. Not enough to be my boyfriend but maybe a little more than a friend. Whatever that means.

I still talk to Demitri almost every night. It's funny because at school we don't talk. We lock eyes from across the room. We smile, wink and blow kisses to one another when no one is watching. But we don't talk. It's different outside of school. We talk every night, go on dates and we even kiss. A lot. He hasn't asked me to be his girlfriend. I don't know why he hasn't. I'm definitely not asking him and I'm also not going to assume that we are together.

Usually, I would be out with him on this beautiful Sunday afternoon. He's out of town and Trey is off with one of his girlfriends so Lola is my next friend of choice for the day.

"I see you and Mike have been spending a lot of time together" Lola said to me out of nowhere, interrupting my thoughts. I detect a hint of jealousy and wondered where it was coming from. She's been encouraging me to get with him since the day I gave him my phone number. Maybe I'm tripping. Maybe it's not jealousy I hear in her voice.

"Yeah so? So do you and I. Because we're friends."

"Yeah, but that's different." I don't think the sound is jealousy. Maybe just thoughtful.

"How is that different? Half of the time you're with us." I say still trying to figure out where she was going with this.

"Yeah, but what about the other half? Girl I need the tea and you're holding back".

"That's because there's nothing to tell." I try reassuring her. I haven't told her about Demitri so she has not idea that it's him who I've been hanging out with so much. I also let her go off of what she sees with Mike so she's pretty much clueless.

"Well, if you ask me friends don't kiss" she rolled her eyes.

"Well, I dramatically dragged out my l's, nobody asked you. And anyway, as far as you know we don't kiss, you're just making assumptions" I said with an attitude.

I couldn't believe she was accusing me of lying to her. I am, but still. If I were dating Mike, she'd be the first to know. After all she is always around. And I do stress always. As far as kissing goes, I still haven't told her anything about that or anything else and this little rant of hers lets me know that I'm doing the right thing. She don't need to know all of my business. I don't know what's happening. I used to be able to tell Lola everything, but

Trey may be right, I have to look at her a little more closely now.

"Hey Goddess. Lady Lola, how are you? Mike greeted us on my front porch. He noticed the look on Lola's face and asked, "What's wrong Lola?"

"Nothing. Everything is fine" she responded.

"What's wrong with her?" he asked ignoring her response.

"Oh, it's not you, it's me", I said.

"Well, it might actually be you too" I wrinkle my forehead unsure of what was really going on with Lola.

"Me too huh?" he asked with raised eyebrows. That's not exactly how I thought he would respond. Lola seemed to not expect him to respond at all. With a bit of a surprised she said

"Yeah, you too. I was just asking our girl here what's up with you two and she's trying to tell me you're just friends".

"Well, we are just friends", he shrugged.

"Oh shut up" she said quickly before he could say anything else, "Friends don't kiss" she snapped.

"Well" he shrugged, "we don't kiss." I mean I want to."

Yes. He can keep a secret. The celebration in my head was lit until he turn to me, grab my face and kiss me. I can't help it. I kiss him back but then I push him away.

"I hope she lets me do that again" he's looking at me and smiling. "She's good at it". His eyes still locked into mine and then break off to look at Lola. I don't know how to respond. I'm shocked. I did not expect him to do that. I'm a little upset he did it in front of Lola but that feeling is outshined by the feeling in the pit of my stomach and the feeling in between my legs. I blink back flashbacks from the photography room and try to focus on what's happening right now.

"Look it's no secret that I'm into Lorde but we are not dating. We're just friends."

"What? But you're together all the time."

"No, we aren't" he said with a frown, "you're always around. Always" he says with big eyes. "We don't hang out without you", he said pointing to her. She turned and looked at me in disbelief.

"You said I was only there half of the time." "Yeah, he picks me up first and drops me off last so" I shrugged, "technically that's pretty accurate."

"Tech- Lorde really? You were just going to let me act crazy over nothing?" I give her a blank stare before answering.

"No, you were getting yourself worked up all on your own. I told you we were just friends. You've never seen us kiss even one time and you assume that we always do it." I thought for second.

"Even if I did kiss Mike, so what if we kiss? Why are you so worried about it?" Now I'm certain it was jealousy that I heard earlier. It wasn't concern or thoughtfulness. Trey is right. She really is jealous of me. *Wait until I tell him about this shit.*

"I guess I'm just jealous. I always feel like a third wheel."

"Well stop third wheeling it Lola. You have a boyfriend. I don't like him, but he is…yours" I say unable to find anything nice to say about him. I don't know what is going on in her mind. Maybe she has a crush on Mike and doesn't want to say anything.

"What?" I shrug. "You want to kiss him too? Go for it." I say pushing her close to Mike.

"No thank you" Lola said with a disgusted look on her face.

"First of all, it's rude to talk about me like I'm not standing right here. Secondly, damn you just gon' let her kiss me like that? And you. Why do you look so disgusted?" There was a long pause and then we both started laughing uncontrollably. Mike stood there for a second looked back and forth between me and Lola and then shook his head. "Are y'all done yet? Let's go".

"Let's go?" We stop laughing.

"Go where? We ask in unison.

"Well, I have a surprise for who I thought was a friend, Lola. Now I'm not so sure that she even wants to be my friend".

"Lola is your friend." I defend her. I really want to ask why it's her he has as surprise for.

"Yeah, you cool or whatever" she said rolling her eyes and smiling at Mike.

"Aww you know you're my li'l homie" he said playfully putting her in a headlock and giving her a noogie.

"Stop boy you gon mess my hair up" she said slipping under his arm and fixing her hair.

"So, what's this surprise? I ask trying to mask my attitude.

"Dang nosey. It's for Lola, not you."

"I still want to know." I put my hands on my hips.

"Wait you didn't tell Lorde?" Lola cut in

"No Lola. It's not for Lorde and I knew she'd open her big mouth to tell you. It's a surprise now will both of you get in the car?" he said, opening up the both the back and front passenger doors."

"Where are we? Lola asked as we pulled into our destination.

"My house. There's someone I want you to meet."

"Mike don't be trying to hook me up with your brother or none of your cousins or friends. We're cool and all, but no." Lola stopped in her tracks.

"Lola, what's wrong?" I asked. When she didn't answer I followed her gaze to see what she was looking at. She was looking at her idol.

"Aunt Charlie", Mike said, "this is Lola, my homegirl I was telling you about. Lola this is my aunt Charlie." Lola stood there shocked, unable to move.

"Lola", he nudged her out of her trance.

"Oh my goodness you're Charlotte Sinclair. It's so nice to meet you. You are legendary."

"Yeah, Aunt Charlie, Lola wants to be just like you when she grows up. You're her idol."

"Be like her? No, I want to be her" she corrected him. I will change my name to Charlotte if that's what it takes. As Lola rambles on about what she would do to be Charlotte Sinclair I wonder why Mike is introducing them. I thought he liked me but here he is introducing Lola to family members and fulfilling dreams and shit. I was a little confused when he kissed me in front of her earlier but now, I know that we are definitely just friends. Nothing more. Charlotte Sinclair raises a hand to silence Lola.

"I have time to teach you to be like me if you're interested and have time for an internship. It doesn't pay money but" she shrugged.

"Oh I have time" she interrupted. "I definitely have time. Thank you so much."

"You're most welcome dear. It's always refreshing to meet such a young person who has already found their passion. I'm sure you'll be my most remarkable student. Being like me isn't going to be easy and neither will be being you. I just need you to be ready. I have to go, but here's my card" She handed Lola her business card. "Give me a call on Monday after school. I'd like to meet with you and your parents. Enjoy the rest of your weekend guys". Lola can barely keep her composure.

"You are officially my best friend" she says to Mike. "Don't worry Lorde you're more like my sister" She always tells me that I'm her best friend, but I didn't know she meant like sisters.

"Oh, I'm not worried" I say smiling. "I know he can't take my place."

"Oh my goodness guys. I'm going to be working with Charlotte Sinclair! I'm sorry about earlier Lorde."

"Excuse me ma'am, but it doesn't exactly scream friends when a guy takes you to meet your idol." I mocked her.

"Yeah, but that's different. My idol is his aunt. He was just being a good friend."

"Yeah right. He's being a guy. If he didn't like you, he wouldn't have done it." I tease. I may be hating just a little.

"Well, you have to like someone to be their friend so yeah. I guess he does like me. Don't you Mike?"

"You're okay" Mike responded from the driver's seat. He didn't say anything else. He just kept driving.

The whole ride to her house Lola talked about how great it was going to be working with Charlotte Sinclair. She practiced her telephone voice a few times and when she got out of the car, she practiced her 'I work with Charlotte Sinclair' walk. As we pulled off, I was thinking about earlier. Lola wasn't jealous, she just wanted real answers and now I think I do to. If he likes me he needs to say something and now is the time.

"Are you really ok with us being just friends?"

"As long as you keep letting me kiss you I am."

"So if I kiss someone else you wouldn't be upset?"

"Well," he thought for a second, "I'd be sure to do a better job next time so you wouldn't want to do it again, but no I don't think I'd be upset if you told me you did". He doesn't ask if I do.

"What if you saw it?"

"What's this all about?" He asked wondering where this line of questions was going.

"Nothing, just curious".

"We both know what happens when you get curious don't we?" He looks over at me. "Do you want to kiss someone else? I mean it's ok if you do."

"No" I sigh, tilting my head to the side. My thoughts flash to Demetri. Those thoughts fade quickly. He's cute and he's a good kisser, but that's it. The idea of him is fun, but being around him is merely something to do. Mike on the other hand. Well the boy keeps me on my toes that's for sure.

"Ok what's up? Talk to me."

"So what if I stop letting you kiss me?"

"Then I would know that you had a boyfriend."

"And you wouldn't be upset?"

"No. We've already established the kind of relationship we have".

"Hmm. Interesting." It's not exactly the answer I wanted, but it's the answer that I was looking for.

"Look Goddess, if you're trying to change the rules to this thing just tell me. Let me know what's up. We're friends because that's what we said we'd be. Really it's what *you* said we'd be".

"No, I'm not changing the rules."

"Good. So you'll still let me kiss you?"

"I never let you kiss me in the first place" I smirked.

"You never stopped me either. Except that one time but yeah".

"Because you're just so damned good at it" I said kissing him. "And you're right. There is no kissing when I have a boyfriend."

"Chiiilll", he sang, "I know you're not that kind of girl".

"You have no idea what kind of girl I am" I kissed him again. I don't even know what kind of girl I am so it's impossible for him to know.

"So, are you ready to tell me what this is all about? Or are you just going to keep evading the question until I drop it?"

"I think I'll keep evading until you drop it" I said looking at him out of the corner of my eye.

"Ok I see. You got a new boyfriend and thangs" he smiled. "So, tell me who it is" he nudged my arm.

"Don't worry about it. I don't have a boyfriend".

"You damn right he's not your boyfriend" he said pulling me close to him "because I have you at least until graduation".

"What you mean you have me until graduation? You're not my boyfriend either." I sit up and look at him with wide eyes and raised eyebrows.

"I may not be your man but I'm claiming you." He smiled a devious but contagious smile and leaned over to get close. He pulled over and stopped the car. He looked over at me, leaned in even closer and kissed me. He was right. He definitely has a kiss that make me not want to kiss anyone else. It sent a wave through my body and left me a little dizzy. I think about that kiss for the rest of the night. I didn't want Mike as a boyfriend, but I was definitely going to keep kissing him. That doesn't mean that he's the only one I'll be kissing. *Does that make me a hoe? Can you be a virgin hoe?*

Chapter 8

I awakened to my phone ringing. I ignored the call. Who would call me this early? My alarm hasn't even gone off yet. I look at the time. It's 3 am. My phone rings again. This time I look at it. It's Lola. My eyes snap back shut.

"Hey girl you good?" I answer.

"No. I am not good. I am not good at all." Lola said in a panic.

"What's wrong girl." I sit up with eyes still closed. My body threatens to fall back to the bed.

"I need you to come and get me." I can hear her sniffling

"Come and get you?" I repeat her request in disbelief. "Where are you?"

"I can't tell you. I mean you can't tell anyone where you're going".

"Lola where are you?" I growl

"I'm supposed to be at your house".

"Lola you are so lucky I can't yell right now. Where are you?" I demand.

"I'm at Chris's house."

The ride home started out as a quiet one. I looked behind me to find Trey giving Lola an evil glare. I decided not to ask Lola about it around him. She wasn't too happy to see Trey with me when I pulled up.

"So Bobblehead" Trey said breaking the silence. "Why are we picking you up at this hour? And from the so-called ex's house? And why have you been crying?"

"Trey" I say "Let the girl breathe a little before you do that".

"Before I do what?" he challenges

"Before you get on my damn nerves" Lola snaps at him.

"Nah lil girl you don't get to snap at me. I'm the only reason your ass is being saved right now. You know Lorde wasn't coming without me. Now talk".

"Yeah, and I'm sure it took a lot of convincing" she snapped again.

"Trey", I sigh.

"No Lorde. We need answers. Lola refused to say anything else she was mute all the way back to my house.

"I think you should call her parents" Trey said as we sat on the porch. Lola had already gone inside.

"Something isn't right. Don't get caught up in her bullshit. We get in enough trouble by ourselves. We don't need her. You don't need her" Trey urged.

I know he's right but for some reason I'm drawn to Lola. I also feel like something is about to happen. I just don't know what it is or if it's good or bad. As we sit and talk, I tell him about my day with Mike and Lola. He does not seem surprised by anything I say. He's definitely an I told you so kind of guy and I can see the struggle he is having trying not to say it. It is entertaining to watch. It would be even more entertaining if I wasn't on the other end of it.

"Ok so I just made Trey, one of our friends, sneak out to come and get you. We don't have to talk about it, but you have to tell me something"

"Well, she sighed, I have my internship interview today and I look like yesterday.'

"That can be fixed but changing the subject doesn't tell me anything. If I'm going to be sneaking out to get you, I should at least know why."

"Can we talk about this later Lorde?"
I know she is exhausted, but I don't care.

"No, we can't talk about this later. I snuck out of the house. I stole my parents car to drive and get you. Mind you I can barely drive and you think we're going to talk about this later? I've already waited long enough. Now tell me what's up."

"Lorde really?" Lola whined.

"You know what no. You don't have to tell me anything, but you do have to do me a favor."

"What's that?"

"Don't call me the next time you find yourself in this unspeakable situation. Find someone else to call," I said. "I can't hold you down if I don't know the truth."

"What do you mean Lorde?"

"I mean that if something happened to you while you were supposed to be with me, who do you think your parents are looking to for answers. What am I supposed to tell them, but the truth?"

"Lorde I'm going to tell you what happened. I just need a minute."

"Yeah a minute. The amount of time it takes to figure out you're lying and you'd rather I took the fall for what happens than you take responsibility for your own actions."

"Lorde really? Bitch please. I take responsibility for my actions. If it was so serious that I can't take a moment to process shit going on in my life then why the fuck did you come?"

"Because I'm your friend!" I yell.

"Well right now I need my best friend. I'm going to get enough shit from my parents I don't need it from you."

"Well, you say you need your best friend, but you can't even be honest with me. What do you need me for? An alibi? A ride? Bitch please." I roll my eyes. "I should have dropped your ass off at home".

Chapter 9

I need someone to talk to and since I am currently
not speaking to Lola, Trey has to be subjected to me talking
to him about boys. Good thing he doesn't mind. Lately he's
been preoccupied with his girlfriends. He never keeps one
for more than two weeks. I don't know why they don't
notice his pattern. His phone goes to voicemail, but I don't
leave a message. He'll call back when he's free. Demitri is
good at making me feel better so I give him a call. He's
doesn't answer either. Mike has been nowhere to be found
for a while, so I don't bother reaching out to him. I was
invited to a party earlier this week by a friend from school.
I had no intentions of going, but I don't have anything else
to do so, why not? I get dressed and go.

When I get to the party it's in full swing. I
immediately get pulled onto the dance floor by some girls
from school. I am having so much fun. I didn't know that I
like to dance. I also didn't know that I am actually good at
it. I try to dance my frustrations away.

"I didn't think you'd come" the girl who invited me
said. I talk to her every day and I have no idea what her
name is. I'm not sure she ever even told me what it is.

"Of course, I told you I'd be here" I smile. We talk
for a while and I learn her name is Briana when a

newcomer to the party walks up and join our conversation. Briana introduced the newcomer as Chantel.

"Where's Mary? Chantel shouts over the music"

"I don't know. She's somewhere around here. Let's go find her". Mary takes one of my arms and link it into hers. Chantel takes my other arm and does the same. Together they lead me around the party looking for the girl Mary. I don't know that many people at the party but everyone there seems to know who I am.

"Hi Lorde" people spoke to me as we walk through the party looking for the girl Mary. We find her on the steps talking to a boy I recognize from Earth Science. I don't remember his name. I'm not very good with names, but I never forget a face and I always know who you are. Just no names. I was happy I came to the party. It's just what I needed to release. It's the perfect way to recharge for tomorrow.

~ ~ ~ ~ ~

My day was going so smoothly then BOOM!

"Hey Goddess" he says from behind me.

"Don't you hey Goddess me", I say turning around and rolling my eyes at Mike.

"Huh" he said looking confused. "What's wrong with you?"

"Nothing is wrong with me boy. What's wrong with you?" I say pushing his chest.

"Uh nothing?" he said sounding unsure.

"Oh there's something wrong with you. Why is it that every time I start to like you and decide to give you a chance you disappear on me? Then you have the nerve to pop up talking about 'hey Goddess' like shit sweet."

"Well, I had college tours to go on." He looked at me through squinted eyes like he was trying to see through me.

"Then say that. Don't just drop off the face of the earth like you did." I put my hands on my hips. He stood there surprised for a moment and then said

"I didn't. And why didn't you call me Lorde? If you wanted to talk, why didn't you call me?" He smirked. "My phone was on. I had service", he shrugged, "why didn't you call me?" I picked up his hand and looked him in the eye

"The same reason you didn't call me to tell me you were leaving and the same reason you didn't call while you were gone", I said releasing his hand and walking away. *I can't believe this boy* I think, shaking my head.

"I didn't drop off. I just told you I went out of town. Both times. This time and last time" he said calmly as he followed me down the hall. I didn't stop. I didn't turn around and I refused to answer him. I ignored Mike for the rest of the day. I acted like he didn't even exist. He probably won't talk to me tomorrow, but oh well. He wanted to be a ghost, so I have decided that I shall treat him like one. I. Don't. See. Him.

"Lorde Alexander" an unfamiliar voice broke me away from my thoughts. I looked around to see who it was.

"Hey pretty lady" Brian said as he approached me. I was still a little upset about Mike when I responded.

"Do you even go here? The only time I see you is in the hall trying to get my attention every once in a while."

"Uh did I do something wrong?" he held his hands up in surrender

"I don't know. Probably. You tell me." I snap at him.

"Ok", he smiled. "How about we meet up after school and talk about it?"

"Meet up after school? I don't know you. I don't even know your last name", I said putting my hands on my hips.

"Dixon" he said without hesitation. "My name is Brian Dixon". I tried to hold back a smile, but I failed then

I thought about his name. Dixon. Why does that name sound so familiar to me?

"Alright Dixon. After school."

"Cool. Meet me in the parking lot. I'll be waiting for you" he said touching my chin and winking at me.

I didn't see Brian again so when school let out I had already made up my mind that I wasn't meeting him in the parking lot. Turns out I didn't have to. He was waiting for me outside of the front doors of the school.

"Hey pretty lady" he said with a smile.

"Hello Brian Dixon" I say suppressing a smile.

"You ready to go?"

"Go? I raised my eyebrows. "I never said I was going anywhere with you".

"You didn't have to. You agreed to meet me at my car, so it was kind of implied."

"Sorry for the miscommunication, but Brian Dixon, I don't know you."

"Well Lorde Alexander, I was planning to change that today. Let's go."

I consider refusing to get into the car but before I could refuse again he grabbed my hand and led me to his car. I saw Lola, but turned my head before she could see me as he opened the door for me to get in. I got in feeling a little adventurous. I've never done anything like this before. I typically don't do things without telling at least Lola what I'm doing. I knew it was potentially dangerous but still. I welcomed the action. I was due for a little danger anyway. I mean I have to live a little right? I can't live my life in the bubble my parents want me to all of my life. Ok I'm not *that* brave. I shoot Trey a t text telling him what I was doing. He sent back the emoji of the man slapping his forehead.

Chapter 10

Lola keeps calling me, but I keep ignoring her. I haven't been speaking to her and she's only calling to find out who I just got in the car with.

"Who you duckin' so hard?" Brian asked.

"Oh, it's nobody. Don't worry about it' I say trying to brush it off.

"Oh, it's somebody. And they're trying real hard to get your attention. So", he shrugged, "who's my competition".

"Oh you have plenty of competition, but that's not who is calling" I say with a wink.

"Ok" he chuckles.

"If you must know" I say before he can continue, "it's my friend, Lola."

"Damn girl why you duckin' your bestie?" he says not taking his eyes off the road.

"Bestie?" I chuckle

"What you don't like my word choice."

"No. I hate the word bestie." I said bluntly. "Aren't we supposed to be getting to know one another?" I ask trying to change the subject.

"You're right. That's the goal." We look at each other and smile for a moment.

"So, Mr. Dixon tell me something about yourself."
I turn in my seat so I can face him.

"Ok. Well, first off Mr. Dixon is my grandfather.
You can call me"

"-Brian Dixon" I interrupted. I'll just keep calling
you by your name.

"Or you can call me Trey like everyone else does".
Trey, another familiar name. There is no way I'm calling
him that. I had already decided to call him by his
government name. Besides, I already have one of those.

"Trey? Where did you get Trey from? Your middle
name?"

"No, I'm Brian Dixon the third. I've been called
Trey all my life."

"I don't like it"

"Well", he shrugged, "it's not for you to like but for
you to respect".

"No, the name your mother gave you is the one for
me to respect. My best friends name is Trey so I won't be
calling you that. Less confusion that way"

"How? It's not like I'm ever going to be around the
guy." I look at him.

"You know what? you're right. You and I probably
won't be friends that long."

"Yeah alright" he chuckles "we'll see"

"You like how I say your name. You like how
smoothly it rolls off my tongue."

"You right" he looks over at me and licks his lips "I
do like it" he looks back at the road.

"So Mr. d-" I stop, clear my throat and continue.
"Dixon, where are you from?" He looked at me for a
moment before he answered

"Miami".
We talked for half an hour before I realize that he hasn't
stopped anywhere yet.

"Don't get me wrong the conversation is cool and all, but where are you taking me?" I was lying. The conversation was not good. It was generic and I didn't really care to have it anymore.

"Nowhere", he replied, "just driving" he said looking over at me and smiling.

"What? You think I'm kidnapping you shorty?"

"No that's not a fear of mine. I mean I don't know you like that. But just know that if you are I will be found, and you will die."

"Damn girl, you threatening me already?" "No threat. You're new around here so I doubt you know much about the Alexanders."

"Your family name travels further than you think. Your mom is legendary, and your dad is a god. Even you Princess Lorde Alexander. With both your parents being doctors, I'm sure you know how to kill someone and make it look like an accident"

I smirk a little. "Only you know who you really are."

"The rest of us just know what we see and believe whatever we hear" he finishes my sentence looking over and flashing a gorgeous, blinding, white smile. That got my attention. My daddy says that to me all the time. Brian Dixon just quoted my daddy. I have to do some real research.

"Where did you say you were from?"

"Miami."

"Oh. How long have you been here?"

"Since school started."

"It's crazy it took me this long to notice you. What brought you here?"

"You know you sound like a nosey old lady", he said with raised eyebrows.

"Oh sorry. I was just trying to get to know you."

"Yeah, well it feels like an interrogation."

"How do you know what an interrogation feels like?" He started to answer but instead he stopped talking and pulled over. I laugh nervously.

"What are you doing?" I look over to see that he is just staring at me.

"So, are we going somewhere or are you taking me home?"

"What's up with you Lorde?" He's not in the mood for the hard time I'm giving him.

"Nothing. I just don't think I'm interested anymore." He read right through my attitude.

"Oh you're interested. What's really up?"

"No, I don't think I am. I'm not into anyone who thinks they have a reason to lie to me or anyone who thinks I'm dumb enough to not know what is happening."

"Girl what you talkin' about? I'm not lying to you."

"Ok Mr. 'I asked around about you but only asked your name', it's really strange that you already know so much about me when I know so little about you. We're supposed to be getting to know one another so when you're ready to really tell me about yourself then you know what's up. Now take me home", I demand. I didn't tell him where I live and I didn't give him directions. When we pull into my driveway and he gets ready to get out, I turn and ask

"Brian?"

"What's up?" he said sounding exhausted.

"How do you know where I live?"

He looked at me and shook his head and got out of the car. He walked around and opened my door for me.

"Thanks".

"You're welcome." He walked me to my door and my dad was sitting on the front porch.

"Brian. My man. What's up witcha?"

"Wassup boss man."

This can't be happening. I'm finally in high school and able to date. How did my dad find a way to interfere?

"Wait a minute. Boss man? My man? Daddy really? This is some bullshit!"

"Watch your mouth", Brian interrupts. "Bitch shut up. Don't tell me what to do." "Watch your mouth" my dad says.

"Daddy!"

"Don't daddy me after you just cursed at me. You know what's up. Express yourself but with respect."

"I'm sorry Daddy. But I'm not dumb and both of you tried to play me today."

"Play you? You know I'd never try to play you".

"Then why him?" I asked pointing to Brian.

"Lorde, I just know his parents. I didn't know that you know each other too."

"Yeah right, Daddy you got the boy out here quoting you." I cross my arms and shift my weight to one leg.

"Look, Brian here just moved in across the street. Brian and his family are new in town. I don't know what this is" he said pointing back and forth between Brian and me "but I don't have anything to do with it baby girl and I'm not letting you drag me into it. Now excuse me while I go freshen up my drink". He kissed my forehead and went into the house. I look at Brian.

"I really did only know who you were after I asked around" he said.

"Yeah right, liar. When you're ready to talk, you can hit me up. I'm sure you have my number already" I say. "You seem like the type he'd find."

"Well it's a good thing you found me first" he said with a gorgeous smile. I wasn't about to fall for that though. Gorgeous smiles seem to be my weakness.

"Yeah, but I didn't", I say stepping into the house, but not going all the way in.

"Wait Lorde. I don't have your number."

"Well since you are so acquainted with my father, I'm sure you know how to get it."

"Yeah, I do", he said. He didn't show it but I could tell he was getting annoyed. "When you want something you either ask for it or take it" he said approaching me. "Now I've already asked for it. You gon give it to me or do I have to take it?" He snatched my phone out of my hand and tried to call himself. I snatched it back not breaking eye contact. "You know how to get at me when you're ready to stop lying to me" I say and walk up the steps. "You live across the street remember".

"I didn't lie to you." He pleaded.

"Whatever boy bye." I step the rest of the way into the house and close the door.

~ ~ ~ ~ ~

I put my bag down and check my phone. Twelve missed calls and four text messages from Lola. Two calls and one message from Mike. I'm not talking to Lola. I'm only halfway talking to Mike, so I decided to see what he wanted first. Before I could call, my dad entered my room.

"We need to talk."

~ ~ ~ ~ ~

As soon as I'm done talking to my dad, I pick up the phone and call Lola. I didn't want to. I just had to find out why she was being so dumb.

"Hello" she answers.

"Bitch really? You gon call my daddy?" I ignore her greeting.

"Hell yeah" she said unapologetically. "You got in some dudes car and ain't say shit. We don't know him!"

"No Lola, you don't know him. I know him just fine."

"Bitch, no you don't." Lola's voice is full of doubt

"Yes I do. You don't know him. And are you sure you want to play this game with me? I can still call your parents about that fucked up ass Chris. I have plenty to tell them."

"You don't even know what happened."

"I don't need to know. I know you're a dumb, pressed bitch and I know the details of every other time I had to save your dumb ass from him."

"Really Lorde?"

"Bitch, try me."

"Damn Lorde I was just worried about you. I called and texted you several times and you didn't answer me. We don't do that, even if we are mad at each other. What was I supposed to think? What was I supposed to do?"

She was right, but I wasn't about to let her know that. She may have been right, but we also don't call parents unless it's a real emergency. A rule she begs me to break for her and I always do, but she never does for me.

"You know damn well we beefin' right now. You also know that I'm not about to put myself in danger. You did that dumb shit on purpose."

"Well bitch if we wasn't talking then, we are now" Lola attempted to laugh it off.
Who does she think she is? She wronged me. She doesn't' get to decide when I'm ready to talk to her.

"No. We're not. Not until you stop lying to my face. You weren't worried about me. I was obviously ignoring your calls. You were just being shitty and trying to get me in trouble, but it didn't work. Now it's my turn".

"Lorde, No! I swear if you tell my parents anything, I'll never talk to you again."

"Well, it's been a good run. You want to stop being my friend for potentially saving your life then oh well."

"That's not why you're doing it. You're doing it to be a bitch". I could hear her trying to hold back tears.

"You know what? I actually care about your life. Even if you don't care about it yourself. And I may be a bitch, but I'm not your bitch. Bye Lola." I hang up before she could say anything else ridiculous. Why is everybody lying to me today? Is it lie to Lorde day?

Chapter 11

As soon as I hung up on Lola, Mike called.

"What?" I answer.

"Well hello to you too. What are you doing?"

"What do you want Mike?"

"Why have you been ducking me all day?"

"Because Mike, I'm not fucking with you right now. I'm tired of everybody thinking they can deal with me on their terms. You and Lola included. You disappear every time I show interest."

"You already yelled at me for that. What's going on with you and Lola?"

"Me picking her up all hours of the morning from Chris's house. She still hasn't told me anything and she expects me to keep all her shit under wraps. Then she had the nerve to call my dad and snitch on me after swearing me to secrecy. Fuck that raggedy bitch."

"Snitch on you? About what?"

"The bitch mad because I know people that she don't know."

"Oh, ok I see. This is about the mysterious Brian. Lola doesn't know that he's who you left with today."

"Wait a minute. How did you know I left with someone today?" I smirked.

"Look Goddess I'm always going to make sure you're straight".

"Yeah right"

"What? You thought that since we're just friends that I'm not still checkin' for you?"

"Actually, that's exactly what I thought. Why would I think anything else?"

"Goddess I'm feeling you like a motherfucker and that ain't gon change. So yeah, like I said, I'm always going to make sure you're straight."

"Thanks Mike." That's all I could think of to say. *Really Lorde, that's all you got? He pours his heart out and all you have to say is thanks. You're better than that.*

"Goddess baby you don't have to thank me." Just then Trey called on the other line. I was relieved because I needed to talk to someone who understood me about Lola and who better than my lifelong best friend.

"Let me call you back Mike".

"Alright don't forget about me" he said before hanging up.

"What's up girl you busy?" Trey asked before I said hello.

"Nope. Not at all what's up?"

"I'm about to come through. I gotta talk to you about something."

"You can't talk about it now?"

"No, I need to talk to you face to face Lorde."

"This isn't you trying to fix Lola and me, is it?"

"You'll see when I get there he hung up". He's definitely about to try to fix me and Lola. I don't know why. He doesn't even like her like that. He never did.

"Hello house Alexander" Trey says as his way of acknowledging everyone as he walks in without knocking.

"Hey there handsome" my mom said grabbing his face and kissing his forehead.

"Trey my boy" my dad said, let me holler at you for a moment."

"I came by to talk to Lorde. Do you mind if I holler at her first and swing by before I go?"

"Oh yeah, no rush". He grabs my arm and lead me up the stairs and to my room. When we got to the room he started talking immediately. He needs an alibi to get out of going somewhere he doesn't want to go with a girl he don't want to go with as usual. I thought he came to talk to me about Lola but that is not the case. After solving his girl problems I tell him about what happened with Lola and asked him his thoughts.

"Why the hell do I care about bobblehead ass Lola? I told you to get rid of that chick. Talking about she's your best friend. That girl ain't nothing but trouble." He held his hand out and waved it in front of me

"She crossed enemy lines." I said firmly.

"No she didn't. She didn't cross enemy lines. As much as I hate to say it the bobblehead was looking out for you".

"What?"

"Just hear me out before you spaz. Think about it. She don't know that dude and you leave school with him. And then don't answer no calls or texts. What is she supposed to think? You know you should've let her know you was straight."

"Let her know? I let you know. Why do I need to let her know anything? We aren't speaking. She had the nerve to call my dad!"

"Called your- OH HELL NAW!" Trey heard how loud he was and lowered his voice. "She crossed the line". He didn't lower his voice soon enough because my mom yells from wherever she is in the house.

"WATCH YOUR MOUTH IN MY HOUSE!"

"YES MA'AM" We call back in unison and then continue on with our conversation.

"It's like she's out for blood, but why? It's fucked up. I didn't snitch on her ass".

"Perhaps you should have, but it's too late for that now. Let it go and let her go." I suck my teeth and roll my eyes.

"How about ice cream? You down for some ice cream right now?" he asked trying unsuccessfully to hold back a smile.

"I'm always down for ice cream." Then I thought about it and said "Trey?"

"What's up?"

"Thank you."

"Don't thank me if you're going to end up being her friend again. Thank me when it's really over" he chuckled. "I'm going to talk to your pops really quick and we can go.

"Hey Goddess" Mike said as I was ordering my ice cream. Trey turned to see Mike approaching. He rolled his eyes and turned back to the counter.

"Hey Mike" I said turning and hugging him and being unexpectedly kissed on the lips. "You know what? On second thought I'll take that second scoop I said with a smile to the girl behind the counter". Trey's phone rang and he looked at me. I knew it was his mom and that he had to get home immediately. I'm not ready to go. I look back at Mike as he looks at the menu.

"Go I'll catch a ride with Mike" I whisper. He kisses my forehead and mouths thanks and darts out of the door.

"And I'll have whatever she's having" Mike said hugging me from behind.

"How did you know where to find me?" I asked still in his embrace.

"I didn't. I just so happen to run into you as I was getting ice cream" he squeezed me and rocked us from side to side.

"Ok, what's up?" I say turning around and backing him up with a little push. "Talk to me."

"What do you mean?" he faked confusion.

"I mean you're acting out of character. You all extra affectionate and shit. What's up?"

"I can't get nothing past you, I see". He smirks

"Sarcasm is angers ugly cousin"

"There is absolutely nothing ugly about you Miss Alexander".

"Very funny. Don't try to dodge my question. What's up with you? Talk to me".

"Nah not yet. I can't talk about it yet."

"Not even with me?"

"You talk to Lola yet?"

"I am no longer friends with Lola

My phone rings. I look at the caller id and it's my father. I excuse myself to take the call.

"Hey daddy", I answer my phone.

"Lorde, baby girl I need you to meet me at the Bordeaux's, it's important."

"What's wrong? Is everything ok with Lola?"

"Lorde just meet me there" he said and hung up the phone. I asked Mike for a ride.

When I get to Lola's my parents were already there. I knew when I saw both of their cars that this was a bad situation. Something was definitely wrong. *Damn* I thought, *I knew I should've told on this bitch. Trey was right.* Now something bad has happened. I let myself in the house and headed for the family room where I knew I would find everyone. Lola was the first in my line of sight. She sat there with her head down, crying. I stood looking at her for a second then I walked over to her. I kneeled down and lifted her face into my hands. Tears streamed down her swollen face. I began to cry too.

"Lola who did this to you?" I demanded

"I CAN'T BELIEVE THIS BITCH!!! I storm out of the house and get in Mike's car. He was still waiting for me. He didn't come in because he didn't want to get in the middle of things.

"What's wrong?" He asks as I close my door. Before I could say anything Lola opened the door and got in the back seat.

"Lorde, I'm sorry".

"BITCH GET THE FUCK OUT!"

"Lorde please". Tears began to stream down her face again.

"Lola" I say calmly this time." Get the fuck out of my face."

"Lorde."

"WHAT? YOU WANT ME TO CARE ABOUT YOUR TEARS? I DON'T LOLA. I DON'T GIVE A FUCK ABOUT YOUR TEARS. YOU ARE A LIAR AND I HATE YOU!" I scream from the top of my lungs

"Whoa whoa whoa" Mike said taking my hand. "Calm down girl. What's going on?"

"ASK THE DUMB BITCH IN THE BACK!" I snatch my hand back and pointing to Lola.

"Okay, Lola you want to tell me what's going on?" he turned in his seat to look at her.

"Mike right now I just need to talk to Lorde."

"OH NAH BOOBOO YOU HAD YOUR CHANCE TO TALK TO LORDE AND ALL YOU DID WAS LIE. GET OUT!" I shout even louder.

"Lorde."

"Lola" I say attempting to calm myself down, "if I tell you to get out one more time I will go back inside and tell everything I know." I'm taking short and heavy breaths in attempt to keep the tears forming in my eyes from falling.

"Lorde really?

I didn't say anything. I got out of the car and went back into Lola's house to keep good on my word. I told her parents everything. I started from the beginning and when I was done they stared at me in awe. They had no idea how to respond. I didn't give them a real chance to. I just left. I silently got back into Mike's car.

"Want me to take you home?"

"Yes Please". When I get home my parents aren't back yet. Neither of their cars are here. I look across the street and see Brian coming out of the house. He sees me and wave. I don't' wave back I turn and go in the house. When I get up to my room Trey is there.

"What's wrong?"

"I'm here for you. I was here when your parents got the call. I told you that girl was no good." He said standing up and opening his arms. I walk straight into them wrapping my arms around his waist.

"You were here? I thought you went home."

"I did but then we came over here" he shrugged". "You know my moms is crazy. She didn't believe me when I said I was out with you. She thought I was with"

"I know she thought you were with one of your girlfriends. That's because I'm always your alibi."

"No. ok yeah you are. You good though?" he shifted the attention back on to me.

"Hell no I'm not good. When my parents get home I'm going to be in deep shit because of Lola."

"Damn. Do you think you'll still be able to"

"I'm not going to be able to do anything. I'm going to be grounded forever. I'm not going to be able to leave the house until hell freezes over"

"Getting you out of the house is a cake walk."

"Yeah, you get in easy enough" I say motioning to my open window.

"And breaking you out will be just as easy.

~ ~ ~ ~ ~

Seconds after Trey leaves Brian knocks on the door.

"Hey" I say stepping out onto the porch. He doesn't say anything. He just kisses me and leaves. I don't know how to respond. Nothing like that has ever happened to me. Before I got a real chance to process the kiss my parents were walking through the front door. I thought they were going to be upset with me and yell at me for an extended period of time and ground me for like ever. None of that happened. I don't leave the house for the rest of the day. I stay in my room and I don't surface until dinner. I'm too afraid that they'll change their minds and wage war against me. I know I'm being dramatic but trust me I'm not being *that* dramatic. Shortly after I've had dinner Mike shows up. He says he wants to check on me after what happened with Lola earlier.

" You're just in time for dessert. I would actually like to try again with the ice cream now please?

"So how did it go with Brian Dixon?" I detected a little jealousy in his voice.

"How did you know his last name?"

"He asked me about you this morning. That's not all I know about him."

"Oh really? What else do you now?" I know more about Brian than I let Mike believe.

"Don't worry about that. Answer my question first. How did things go?" I wonder why he took so long to ask me about it but I leave it alone.

"They went ok, I guess. Nothing special. Just a ride home." I wasn't about to give him details about my ride with Brian, especially knowing how he feels about me. He keeps telling me he's feeling me even though he won't ask me to be his girlfriend. He couldn't possibly expect details.

"Just a ride home huh?" he looked unconvinced

"What? You want details?" I raise my eyebrows

"Yeah", he shrugs.

"No", I shrug.

"Why not?"

"Because it's none of your business. You don't get to ask me about that. You don't get to ask me about boys."

"Oh, my bad. I thought we were friends."

"Oh, we're friends, but considering the kind of friends we are, we don't talk about boys."

"Oh yeah? I talk to you about girls. What kind of friends are we?" He said moving to my side of the booth.

"I don't know" I say nervously, "we're just friends." He laughs.

"What's so funny?" I try not to sound offended, but I don't like the idea of him laughing at me.

"I like you Goddess. You're not like other girls. You're a real one". He locks his eyes into mine

"What do you mean?" I keep his gaze

"I mean you keep it real no matter what. You not out here faking. You not claiming no fake brothers or fake cousins. Boys are boys, friends are friends, but me? You have no idea how to classify me other than friend. But we both know this is more than a friendship. I may not be your man, but we both know I'm your man. I don't know how you see things but in my eyes you're my girl". It was a sweet sentiment, but I wasn't feeling it. I am nobody's girl.

"Well the way I see things is exactly what I told you before. We kiss and that's nice. You express how you feel and that's nice. I express a little interest and you disappear without a word. That leaves me confused and open to other boys. So no, I'm not your girl" I shrug.

"You may not think so, but you are" he winks.

"No, I'm not, I chuckled. "Look", I say, "I know you're not used to claiming someone as your girl, but you wouldn't leave me open like that if I were your girl. And if you were my man, you'd know my favorite ice cream" I smiled.

In that moment he realized he had no idea what kind of ice cream I ordered before we had to leave.

"You don't like strawberry shortcake?" he raised his eyebrows.

"Oh, I love it, you'll learn though" I say with a wink and turn away to finally break away from his optic hold.

"So that means you're going to finally stop faking and be my girl?"

"No that just means you're about to learn my favorite icecream", I laugh.

"What's so funny?"

"I'm not about to be one of your girls. I'm not about to be another Mike Sinclair statistic."

"What's that supposed to mean?"

"It means that everybody knows about you and your reputation. You don't do girlfriends. You don't even call girl. You just collect their numbers for your phone.

"That's not true. I call you. I'm trying to make you my girlfriend and you have no good reason to keep telling me no."

"I do have good reason."

"You're not going to be the next Mike Sinclair statistic. You're going to be the girl who kept Mike Sinclair's attention" he's trying to convince.

"Oh yeah, because you're a real prize". I couldn't mask my sarcasm.

"No, but you are. I'm the guy who got and kept Lorde Alexander's attention."

"Don't get cocky. You haven't figured out how to keep my attention yet" I say with a wink. "Let's not forget about Brian" I smirk.

"Oh, I haven't forgotten" he smiles. "And don't think I don't know about that guy Demetri too" . I almost choke on my ice cream. I clear my throat.

"Demitri?" *How does he know about Demitiri? Nobody knows about Demitri. I haven't even been hanging around or even talking to him lately. Now that I think of it I haven't even been seeing him in class.*

"Don't play dumb with me. I know all about him he smiles. "You think I haven't noticed you out and about with him?"

"Stalk much?"

"I'm not stalking you. I just seen you out with him and found out who he was. I told you I'm going to always look out for you. I'm going to always have your back."

Chapter 12

Mike is staying for dinner tonight. He pulled another disappearing act and is just trying to stay in my good graces. I don't know why he cares so much. It's not like we're dating. During dessert there was a knock at the door. My father looked at me as he got up to answer it. I shrugged my shoulders and slightly nodded my head toward Mike. I was hoping like crazy it wasn't anybody for me. I excused myself and followed my dad to the door. It was Lola. I turned to go back into the dining room.

"Lorde", my dad said. I turned back around. He let her in and returned to the dining room.

"I have company" I said going to the door and opening it for her to leave, "I don't want to be rude, so you'll have to come back some other time" I said. She walked out of the door as I guided her and turned around once she was on the porch.

"Lorde please come out and talk to me. I know you have company, so it'll only take a minute." I looked at the girl that I once called my best friend. She couldn't even look at me. I don't know why she wants to talk to me. There is nothing she can say to me that will make me forgive her and I'm really not in the mood to argue with her tonight. Against my better judgement I stepped out onto the porch anyway.

"I just want to say I'm sorry."

"You already said that" I said before she could say anything else.

"Just listen for a minute" she said holding her hand up. "I'm not here for your forgiveness because I know I'm not going to get it."

"Then why are you here Lola? Get to it already. I already told you I have company and I'm not trying to be rude". I know she wanted to tell me to shut up but she didn't. Instead she took a deep breath and continued.

"Look Lorde I just want to make you understand. You can decide what to do after that".

"Look Lola, I don't really have time for that right now. All I can tell you is that I've already made my decision. There is nothing you can say and no level of understanding that will make me forgive you. I've been asking you to tell me something for weeks and you wait until now. I'm sorry but it's too late. I don't want to know. I don't care. We are not best friends." I consider leaving her on the porch, but decided against it. Instead I stood there and waited until she left the porch. She stopped when she noticed Mike's car at the end of my driveway. She looked back at me but she didn't say anything. She just left.

"Everything alright?" My dad asks as I take my seat at the table.

"Fine" I say and take a sip of water. I ask if we can be excused from the table and Mike and I decided to go for a walk around the neighborhood. We walked and talked for about an hour. It was nice to get some fresh air.

"So" I say as we get back to my house and sit on the porch steps "are you going to disappear on me again?"

"Why you ask that?" he chuckles. I look at him with raised eyebrows. He hugged me. "I'm serious" I say slipping out from his embrace. "You have to tell me when you're leaving".

"Ok" he says gently pulling me back into his embrace. "I heard you the first three times you yelled at me about it, and I hear you now." I settled in his embrace before I asked again

"So? Are you about to disappear again?"

"Well," he paused "yeah. I'm not disappearing though." He paused for a moment. "Lorde", he said standing up "you constantly remind me that we can only be friends or whatever it is that we are. We aren't together no matter how bad I want to be. You aren't my girlfriend, and I am not your boyfriend. You can't expect to keep tabs on me. It's time for you to figure out what you want."

"What do you mean? I know what I don't want. I don't want to be another of your conquests that"

"See what I'm saying?" he cut me off. "You're too busy worrying about what other people think. They don't know me. Not like you do. Yeah, I get numbers. Yeah, I get girls. Do you hear me name dropping? Do you see me with a bunch of other girls? No! What you see is me chasing after you every chance I get. You're more worried about other girls than you are me. Forget what people know about me. Consider what you know about me." He is talking way too fast. This conversation is escalating even faster. *Let me hold it together.*

"You're right Mike. All we can be is friends or whatever this is." *That is not holding it together. Come on Lorde. That's not what you meant to say.* My thoughts are going one way and my mouth is moving in the opposite direction. "I can't get past your reputation for us to actually be together.

"I can respect that" he said after taking a moment to think. "It's cool" he said kissing my forehead, "I still got you". He walked me back in the house, said goodbye to my parents and left after kissing me on the forehead again. I am a little shocked by the kiss on the forehead. He has never done that before. *What the hell is that supposed to mean?*

Through all of this drama that's been going on in my life I've managed to keep my grades up, room clean, phone charged and my lip gloss popping. If I can manage all of that then surely, I can manage a boy. Boys aren't usually a problem, but this boy here is nothing but trouble. I take another stroll around the neighborhood to clear my head before I go in and get ready for bed.

Chapter 13

"Today is going to be a great day" I say aloud. "I am following my path to greatness without distraction. Today is going to be a great day. I am following my path to greatness without distraction". I keep saying this over and over until I leave for school. As soon as I step off of my porch, I notice a familiar car. Brian gets out of the car and walks around and open the passenger side door.

"Good morning" he says with a smile. I don't smile back. "Can I take you to school?"

"No thank you" I say not taking a step.

"Come on Lorde" he says "I want to talk to you" he approaches me. "Let me give you a ride to school" he takes my hand in an attempt to hold it, but I don't allow it.

"No thank you" I repeat. He says something else that I don't comprehend because I'm too busy watching my bus pass by, leaving me with no ride to school. I take a deep breath and look back to Brian.

"I know I have some explaining to do and I'm ready now".

"Ok I sigh." He takes my backpack and help me into the car. So much for no distractions. By the time we pull up to school he has earned my forgiveness. He didn't use any gifts or try to sell me a dream like I thought he would. He used that familiarity that he had no idea he had. I was actually surprised. I was even impressed a little.

When I got to class Mike was waiting for me at the door.

"Hey Goddess. I saw you ride out with Brian this morning. I just want to let you know to be careful with that one baby girl."

"Well, hello to you too."

"I gotta get to class. I'll check you later." He kissed my forehead and left me to go into my classroom.

There it is. That forehead kiss again. Why does he keep doing that? What does it mean? And why isn't he kissing me? When I got out of class Mike wasn't there. That's odd because he's always there if he's in school. *He must be falling back* I thought. Instead of going straight to my next class I go and find Mike. I find him outside of his locker. I witness as he turns down an offer from a girl to walk him to class.

"Mike Sinclair", I startle him, and he drops the book in his hand.

"You surprised me girl. What's up?" he picked up his book

"You weren't there to walk me to class so I figured that I'd come walk you to class. He gave a little smile and handed me his book.

"What's up with you?" I demand

"What you mean?

"Why are you acting funny all of a sudden?"

"What you mean? I'm not acting funny".

"What's up with you warning me about Brian?" I look over at him "And that damn forehead kiss, what is that? It's like you switched up on me. Like you're little sistering me or something."

"Lorde" he said stopping and facing me, "you're definitely no little sister of mine. I named you Goddess for a reason. You're my little goddess. And I only kissed your forehead because I know you don't want people thinking we're together." He wrinkled his forehead and shrugged.

"You did it last night too though. And now I'm little? No boo boo, my name is Lorde! Remember who you're talking to boy."

"Calm down" he chuckled. "I told you. You have a lot of growing up to do."

"Don't tell me to calm down. You also said you got me?"

"Yeah. I do have you" he said shaking his head, "and I warned you about your boy."

"Yeah, what's that about?" Mike just looks at me. He serves a straight face as if he wasn't going to dignify me with a response.

"Oh, you don't think I know about Demitri?" I asked. "That boy doesn't even look my way anymore." He blushed a little. "So, what's up?" The bell rang.

"You're late for class" he said.

"Well," I shrug, "walk with me". He kissed me on the forehead and took his book back from me.

"Nope. Get to class Goddess. I'll see you when it's over."

As soon as I step foot into class I hear

"Miss Alexander, we're glad you finally decided to join us."

"Happy to be here" I said taking the first available seat I could find. I look at the clock. *Really teach? Dude, I'm not even late.*

"Pop Quiz!" The teacher announces. I'm glad I attended class. I would have missed the quiz and a project assignment. Mr. Nixon hates repeating himself and he never does. If you're not there or you show up late, you better have a reliable source for information or a doctor's note.

"Glad you went to class?" Mike was waiting for me after class as promised.

"Oh my goodness yes. How did you know?"

"I told you, I got you. You have a lot to learn. You figure out what you want yet?" I know he's referring to our conversation last night but I'm sure I made myself clear.

"I know I want you to take me home today" I say flirtatiously.

"Well ma, Brian brought you to school today. My guess is that he's trying to take you home too."

"Why are you worried about what Brian wants? I'm *your* Goddess". He thought for a second and said,

"I'll swing by your locker when it's time to roll."

"Thank you" I want to squeal but I keep my composure.

"In the meantime," he kissed my forehead, "have a good day". I look around. Just as I thought. We are the only two left in the hallway.

"Again with the forehead kiss?" I shake my head. I stand on my tiptoes and kiss his cheek. "You too"

"Ok, now get to class" he said nudging me in the wrong direction.

"Actually class is this way" I say turning around.

"No" he said spinning me again. "Your class is that way. Now go. I'll see you when it's time to go."

~ ~ ~ ~ ~

When it is time to go Briana, Mary and Chantel rush up to me asking me if I was going to Chantel's party this weekend. I confirmed that I'd be there and asked if she would mind if I brought someone with me.

Interrupting my conversation Lola bumped into me causing my books to fall to the ground. She didn't stop. She didn't apologize. She just kept going.

"You dumb bitch" I yelled out behind her. She didn't turn or say anything back.

"Oh good" Chantel put her hand up to her chest in relief. "I thought you were going to bring *her*."

"No girl I'm talking about Trey."

Her eyes got big as she agreed to my plus one. "We'll see you later girl." As I kneel to pick up my books Mike appears.

"What was that about?" He asked kneeling down to help me.

"Nothing" I say with an attitude.

"Ok" he says taking the hint. "You ready to go?"

~ ~ ~ ~ ~

As I'm finishing one homework assignment and about to start another one my phone rings. I don't answer I just let it go to voicemail. It rings again and it's the same number. This time I answer it. It's Lola. I consider hanging up. but she sounds like she's been crying. I know I should be the last person to give in to her tears, but I just can't help myself.

"What do you want Lola?" I ask trying to mask my concern. I didn't want her to think I actually cared about her tears, especially not after what she did to me.

"Lorde" she said still sniffling. "I need you."

"No, you don't."

"For real Lorde I really do need you".

"Lola", I sigh, "if it's an emergency hang up and dial 911 for any other reason tell me what the hell you want." She continuously tried to suppress her cries but was unsuccessful. I hear it but I am in no mood for it.

"Lola miss me with the tears chick. I've been through enough with you so far and I'm not really ready to go through more with you so call me back when you're really ready to talk. Don't call me for any other reason than that." I was about to hang up, but I heard a loud crash on the other end of the phone.

"Lola" I yell. No answer. "Lola" I repeat "Lola answer me. What happened?" There's still no answer. The phone goes dead. I try calling the number back but there was no answer. I hang up and try again and still no answer. I start to worry and think about where she could be and then I stop. Typically, I would try and handle this myself. but I had to learn from the last time. I couldn't make the same mistake again, so I called her mother. So much for no distractions.

Aaaand they just keep coming. As soon as I hang up with Lola's mom there's an incoming call. I consider ignoring it but I can't because I know that if I do whoever it is will just call again and keep calling until I answer. So I answer it.

"Lorde's drama hotline how may I help you?" I answer sarcastically.

"I call bearing good news" Mike says. I release a sigh of relief.

"Hey Mike. I say. I wasn't really expecting to hear your voice on the other end of my phone so soon. What's up?"

"Why wouldn't you be expecting me? You pretty much told me that this is what was happening".

"Yeah I know. I just thought your stubbornness would kick in and you'd wait until much later."

"Well, who were you expecting? What are in the middle of now?"

"What's that supposed to mean?"

"Nothing" he said.

"No. what is it supposed to mean?"

"It means you're always in the middle of something. Would you like to hear my good news or not?" He said getting impatient. I was going to argue about what he said but I decided against it.

"Yeah, what's the good news?" I ask.

"Come outside. Ride with me. I'll tell you all about it".

"So you just assumed that I'd come outside because you're already here? Didn't you just drop me off? How are you back so fast?"

"Lorde", he sighed "I'm really getting tired of you right now. We were just together little miss 'I want you to take me home' and 'I'm your goddess' he said mocking my voice. "Either come down, ride with me so I can tell you my good news, or I'll go find someone who won't give me a hard time."

"I can't. I have work to do." I say with an attitude.

"Don't forget that I'm not your man. We're friends and if you can't be one then stop making them. Don't forget what we talked about".

"Matter fact you know what? Don't come down. I'm out. When you ready to act like you know what's up then you can come holla at me. Until then be careful out here. Watch out for yourself." He hung up.

Chapter 14

I have been sitting quietly on my bed wondering how things got so heated with Mike. Why did I take my frustration out on him? It was not his fault. He has been a great friend through all of my recent drama. He did not deserve for me to treat him like that. I call to apologize but he sent me to voicemail. I don't leave a message. Instead, I hang up and call right back and he answers.

"Come outside, Goddess".

"No" I say. Come inside Mike. I'm coming to open the door now."

"Your peoples home?" He said not moving from the porch.

"No. why?"

"You sure it's cool for me to be in there?"

"Yeah boy. Why you ask that?"

"Yeah ok". He ran his hand over his head. "The last time a girl told me it was cool for me to be there when her parents weren't it didn't turn out so good. Imma ask you one more time. Is it cool for me to be in there with your parents not home?" I chuckled a little.

"Look Mike. I wouldn't invite you in if I couldn't invite you in. I don't rock like that." He was still a little reluctant, but he sighed and shrugged

"Ok. I just don't want your parents to come home and be surprised that I'm here".

"Of course, they're going to be surprised you're here. It's not like it was planned. They won't be upset though."

"Aight so what's up? Why you want me to come in instead of riding out with me?" He took the closest seat to the door.

"I told you. I have homework to do. I'm not really supposed to be out before it's done."

"Oh, aight well go ahead and get your work done. I can talk to you later. He stood from his chair.

"Or you can relax and talk to me now". I take a seat on the couch and motion for him to join me. He does so nervously. "Loosen up it's just the couch. I haven't even taken you upstairs yet" I pull him down to sit beside me.

"Oh, you're not getting me upstairs."

"Yes, I will. I'm just not ready yet" I flirtatiously nudge his leg with mine. "So, what's this good news you want to tell me about?"

"Oh, that's on hold for right now. I came in for you. We need to talk about something else."

"Ok what's up?"

"You been going through a lot lately and I told you I got you. I didn't have you a moment ago and I'm sorry. It won't happen again. You have enough going on and you don't need me leaving you all confused and shit. But Goddess for real though you need to start thinking of people other than yourself."

"Wow you go from wanting me to figure out what I want to me thinking of someone other than myself?"

"Look Goddess you do need to figure out what you want. That doesn't mean to disregard other people." I don't follow. I feel like he's talking circles around me.

"Ok listen" he takes my hand in his, you can figure you out and at the same time be excited for a friend who just got good news and wants to share it with you first. One has nothing to do with the other. They're just happening at the same time."

"I feel you. It's just that it seems like every time I think of someone else I get fucked over". I lean over and worm my way into his arms. "I'll do better though:".

"You really need to iron that shit out with Lola too. That girl needs you."

"Well, she needs to be real with me. I'm tired of her lying and sneaking around, hiding shit from me. I'm supposed to be her friend and she threw me under the bus not once but twice. She lied on me, lied to me and left me to take the hit. When that didn't work, she tried again."

"What do you mean?"

"That's what happened when our ice cream date got interrupted".

"Ok don't say anymore I don't really want to know. I just need you two to fix it".

"Why are you so pressed for us to fix our friendship?"

"Honestly I don't care if you two are friends or not. All I know is that she is your best friend. and while you are mad at her, you're taking it out on me.

"First of all, Trey is my best friend. Always has been and always will be. Lola was just someone I got too attached to and we are no longer friends.

"Look, Lola is your best friend" he said not at all acknowledging what I just said. I realize in that moment that I never told him that Trey was my best friend and I knew him before he came to our school.

"I don't know what's going on. I don't want to know what's going on. What I do know is that I want my Goddess back because you have been a bitch to me".
I sit up and look at him

"Don't look at me like that. I'm not your man remember. I can say what I want" he winked and pulled me into his arms.

"Yeah, but not that" I snap.

"I'm sorry" he says after a moment of silence. "I don't mean to take my frustration out on you."

"It's cool. Just don't' do it again." I lay still in his arms. I was comfortable there. I felt safe.

"So, are you ready to tell me your good news yet?"

"Oh, you just won't forget about that huh?"

"Nope so you may as well tell me."

"So, you know I've been doing college visits and interviews and stuff right? Or as you like to call it performing disappearing acts"

"Yeah, did you get a response from one of them yet?"

"Actually, yes I did. I got into a few of them with a full ride. I just need to decide which one I want to go to."

"Are they all far away?"

"No not all of them. That doesn't matter though. I'll be home for breaks and you can visit me anytime you want."

"Yeah ok. You say that now. I can visit until you get a girlfriend that says otherwise."

"Goddess chill. You don't have to be jealous of a girlfriend that I don't have yet. Just like I don't need to be jealous of the Brian character. We are what we are, and no one can change that but us."

"Well, we'll cross that bridge when we get there. Congratulations, baby I'm proud of you. And you're right. We shouldn't be in here just chillin with that kind of news. We should be out celebrating. What do you want to do?"

"You, so let's get out of here before we get ourselves into trouble" he said standing up and holding his hand out for me to take it. As we headed for the door my father walked in with Brian behind him.

"Hey Dad"

"Hey little lady where you off to?"

"To celebrate. My boy right here just got into college with a full ride."

"Well, that's definitely a reason to celebrate. Congratulations Mike". My dad said slapping and squeezing his shoulder. "Thank you, sir" Mike's eyes finally left Brian. He had been watching him since they walked in. *So much for him not being jealous of Brian.*

"Come on let's go" I say pulling Mike toward the door.

"Hey Lorde" Brian says.

"What" I turn to look at him.

"I'll be here when you get back" he said with a smile and a wink. I roll my eyes and turn and leave with Mike. I know he is just trying to make Mike jealous

"I don't like that dude" Mike says when we get outside "Be careful with him Lorde."

"I'm not into him" I say. "There's nothing to be careful with",

"Yeah" he paused "you are. It's cool. Just be careful and know that I got you." He looked down. I lifted his chin until our eyes met.

"I got you too" I kiss him.

"And you'll be careful? He looked concerned.

"Yeah, and I'll be careful". It's my turn to look down now. He lifts my chin until our lips meet and he kisses me.

"So where are we going?" I take a deep breath. "How do you want to celebrate?"

"Actually, I think I should go home and tell my parents first. You mind if we do this some other time?"

"I mind a little, but I won't be selfish. It's not about me. It's about you. We can do it some other time". He laughed. It was like he couldn't help it. Then he kissed me. A dizzying kiss that I didn't want to end.

"You are a funny girl. I'll see you later." Mike gets into the car, but he doesn't start it. He just sits there for a moment and he gets out. He walks back up the porch and stand in front of me. "On second thought come on" he says holding his hand out for me to take.

We got pizza and went laser tagging with a few other friends from school to celebrate Mike's accomplishments. After laser tag Mike and I sit in the parking lot for a while talking. We talk so long I almost forget we are in a parking lot. After a while we start kissing. When we came up for air Mike got out of the car. He came around to the passenger side of the car and opened my door. I didn't move. I just sat there. He undid my seatbelt. I sat still. He reached down between my legs. I thought he was going to touch me, but he was adjusting my seat. I gasp as I go sliding backward. He leans my seat back. Not all the way just slightly. He looks around to make sure there is no one around. *Thank God I'm wearing sweatpants today. Good job Lorde,* I think as I lift my butt and he slides my pants down my thighs. He begins kissing me again. This time he trails kisses down my neck. I shiver in excitement of what he will do next. He holds the back of my neck with one hand and with the other he gently inserts a finger inside of me. As I find comfort, he inserts another and now there are two fingers inside of me and I cannot control the explosion that is bound to happen. Then I gasp and my eyes shoot open. Not from release but because he has removed his fingers. He looks around again to ensure that we are still the only ones around. He then dips his head between my legs. His tongue replacing where his fingers once were. *He did not do this last time*. When he's done, he gets up and he pulls my pants back up. He walks around the car and gets in the drivers seat and drive off like nothing ever happened. *Is he serious? Did that just happen? Can it happen again?* He doesn't take me straight home. We ride around for a while in silence. It's not an awkward silence.

It's nice. He holds my hand the whole time. We pull up in front of my house, but I am not ready to go in yet. I also can't stand to be this close to him and not touching him given recent activity. He walks me to the door and kisses me goodbye.

I go back into the house and head straight for the stairs. Before I could get there

"Hey Lorde, back so soon?"

"What do you want Brian Dixon?"

"I told you that I'd be here when you got back"

"So what?" I try shrugging him off. I can't believe he's still here. I have been gone for hours.

"I'm here for you."

"I didn't invite you. You came with my father so you can handle your business with my father and roll out."

"Oh, it's like that? Why is it like that?" he approached me. Backing up, I roll my eyes.

"Oh, that was your dude?" he smiles

"It's like what? Stop just popping up at my house. Try calling first". I realize it sounds ridiculous when I remember that he lives across the street, but I roll with it anyway.

"Was that your dude?" he's still smiling

"None of your business."

"Nah he ain't ya dude."

"Why do you care?"

"You know why I care. I'm feeling you. I need to know who my competition is."

"Come to school more often and you'd know who your competition is."

"Honestly I'm not worried about the competition. All I'm worried about is you. When are you going to let me take you out?

"Is that your way of asking me out?" I look at him with annoyance. His smile faded. I go to the door and open it. "Come back when you figure out the right way to come at me."

"Is that an invitation?" he smiles again.

"An invi- , yes. It's an invitation to leave. I'll see you some other time".

"Yeah, some other time. But I'm not leaving.

"What? Why?"

"I came in with your dad, remember?"

"That was a long time ago" I frown

"We're not done" he shrugs.

Chapter 15

Why is my life moving so fast? and can I slow it down? I think as I take a walk around the neighborhood.

"Hey Lorde." I was snapped out of my thoughts

"Hey Simone" I answer, and she kisses me. Not a friendly kiss on the cheek. She really kissed me. With tongue. And I think I liked it. She kissed me and just walked away. Damn I need to get a grip on my life. The only thing I had good going for me was my grades and knowing I was pretty enough that people wanted to kiss me. I can't figure out things with two boys and now a girl comes and throws my whole shit off by kissing me out of nowhere. At least she was pretty and a good kisser.

"What was all of that about?" Trey said walking up to me.

"You into girls now?" He is exactly the person I needed to see. The very one I needed to talk to. He's always the one to help me get my life back on track.

"I don't know" I shrugged "She just came up and kissed me."

"Out of nowhere"? he looked a little skeptical.

"Yeah." I shrugged again. "She said hey and I said hey and she kissed me."

"Did you like it?"

"I don't know. Are you being a perv?"

"No" he chuckled "just curious" he shrugged.

"What if I said that I did?"

"I'm not here to judge" he said putting his hands up in surrender. "But that may make you a competition of sorts for me. So, what's up with you and that Brian dude?"

"What? You jealous?"

"Nah. I don't do the jealous thing. And why would I be anyway? None of your dudes like me, not the other way around" he chuckled "But that Simone on the other hand" he rubbed his hands together.

"You're such a perv I chuckle."

"Yeah right. You know I've had my eye on that girl".

"Well then I guess that's too bad for you".

"Oh, so you are the competition. Game on Lorde, you're going to give me a better run for my money than any of these dudes up in here".

"Calm down Sparky. I'm not after Simone. Or any other girl for that matter."

"Lorde you're not after anyone. Boy or girl. They are all after you. I don't know when you're going to finally realize that" he chuckled.

"Whatever. Come with me to Chantel's party."

"Yeah cool." He rubs his hands together

"Let me guess. You've had your eye on Chantel too."

"Nah she's cute and all but Mary. Mary is who's on my radar."

"That's too bad. Chantel is really looking forward to your presence. She has a crush on you." He looks like he's giving it some thought. "Look Trey I don't care who you want to do whatever with, but can we please keep my friends off limits?"

"No. Sorry Lorde, but no. Your friends are *too* fine. There's no way I'm not hollering at a girl just because she's one of your friends. You have too many friends for that."

He's right. I do have too many friends for that. On top of that they all want a chance to be with Trey. I don't even bother trying to convince him to change his mind. From what I've seen there is no point because these girls want what they want. I tell him to be careful and leave me out of whatever he has going on with Mary or Chantel or whichever of my friends he's about to pursue.

When Trey and I walk into the party, Chantel greets us at the door. She leads us inside the party and then she takes Trey's hand and head off in the other direction. He turns his head to look back at me. Be careful I mouth to him. I walk around to see who is at the party and I bump into Brian. We dance for a while then we go and talk outside. I decide I'm ready to go but I can't find Trey. I shoot him a text and he tell me he's a little busy and to go ahead and leave without him.

~ ~ ~ ~ ~

He held the door open for me and I got in.

"So, does this mean you're finished being mad at me?" he asked with a charming smile.

"I wasn't mad at you" I said looking away.

"You sure have a funny way of showing it. You seemed pretty mad to me."

We rode for a moment then he broke the silence.

"What's on your mind?"

"I don't know about you" I stopped and thought "I don't know why I need to".

"Because I'm cute" he said rubbing his face.

"You are cute, but that's not it". I stopped talking immediately. I did not mean to say that. He didn't let the silence last long chuckling and shaking his head. He didn't say anything. He didn't look over at me. He just kept driving. Now I know I keep talking about his smile, but behind that smile is a face. A perfectly sculpted face with soul trembling eyes and a mouth made to kiss and never argue with.

"Come on, let's go to my house" I say not looking at him.

"You are trouble" he says shaking his head.

"Not really" I shrug. "I'm just ready to go home. You coming with me or dropping me off?" He doesn't answer.

"We're just hanging out. You know eating, talking, watching TV".

"You really are trouble" he says "I'm not going in there tonight. Not for them to find me there in the morning."

"Who said anything about you still being here in the morning? I'm inviting you to chill not for a sleepover. Relax" He looks over at me but he doesn't say anything.

"If you're scared say you're scared" I say again with a smirk.

"Scared of what? Movies and snacks? Girl you funny. What makes you think I'm scared instead of respectful? Get your mind right" he pointed to his temple, "get your mind right Lorde." I could feel the blood rush to my cheeks, and I knew I was blushing with embarrassment. I take a deep breath and as my face cools I say

"Yeah, ok respectful. You're the same dude who" I stop and sigh "never mind" I shake my head and wave him off. He didn't ask me to continue. We both knew he didn't want me to. I considered doing it anyway but decided against it. Instead, I said

"So will I at least see you later?"

"Yeah, you tryna go to the movies with me?"

"Still trying to get me out on a date?"

"And you're still refusing? You know you're a strange one. You invite me into your house, but you won't go on a date with me?"

"What's strange? I invited you in to kick it. I don't know what you think is going on boo boo, but my intentions are completely pure. I fully expect you to leave my house at a reasonable time. I was just trying to continue to get to know you so I can determine if I'm ready to actually go somewhere with you. Especially with the last mishap still so fresh on my mind. You know what? Don't worry about keeping me company. Someone else can do that for me" I say opening the car door to get out.

"So, who are you going to call to do that?" he asked before I get out.

"It won't be you, so you don't have to worry about it" I say refusing to entertain him any further. He lives across the street. He'll see when they come.

"Alright I'll come keep you company"

"Don't do me any favors." I get out of the car before he can say anything else. He gets out and follows me saying something that I can't really comprehend because my thoughts are too loud. *Why is he so frustrating? Does he have to be so difficult? Do I really need to get to know this guy? I mean it's ok for him to just be the cutie across the street. It's not pertinent that we be friends.* As soon as I close my door there is a loud knock. I open it.

"What did I do?" Brian demanded.

"You're just…you" I move out of the way and let him in.

Chapter 16

Sometimes I wonder how I got to be so damn amazing. I am absolutely amazing. I even amaze myself sometimes. Straight A's on you hoes. Life full of drama and I never skipped a comma. These hoes better take notes.

"Hey Goddess" Mike interrupted my internal gloating.

"Hey boo what's up?"

"Boo? I get to be boo now?"

"Slip of the tongue" I smirk.

"Yeah aiight. I'm about to skate. Do you want a ride home?"

I thought for a second and said "Yeah, I do"

"Aiight grab your stuff. Let's go", he nodded for me to join him. "How's that report card looking though?"

"Straight A's" I say with a clap of my hands and a smile.

"For real? That's awesome. I don't know how you focus on school with your personal life."

"Hey Mikey baby" a girls voice says from behind us. I don't turn to see who it is, but he does. He looks back to me and smile before saying

"Hey Katrina" as we leave the building. She comes out behind us and walks around and ahead of us. She turns and waves and turns back around to leave.

"I think you have a fan. A really big one at that" I chuckle. He looks at me smiles.

"What? You jealous? Can't be with all the fans you have" he winked and nudged me.

"No, I'm not jealous. I'm being supportive. Go get your girl" I wave him in her direction.

"Yeah, but how will you get home? Your bus already left." He looked reluctant to approach Katrina

"I'll be fine. And so will you. She's inviting you to do your Mike Sinclair thing. So, go do it." I give him a light push in her direction.

"Yeah, but I need to make sure you get home."

"Nah I'm good. I'll get home just fine. You're not the only person I know with a car." Just as I said it Brian pulled up to the front of the school. Mike saw him pull up and chuckled

"What? He not your boyfriend yet?"

"Bye Mike" I say pushing him away again, "Go and get your girl". He stands for an extra moment, so I push him in the direction of Katrina, and I head towards Brian.

"Hello Lorde, my lady. How was your day?"

"It was cool" I say not expecting to have to ask what he was doing here since he wasn't in school today. I was glad I didn't.

"I'm here to ask you if I could take you home this afternoon".

"Well, you could have called or texted that" I smile.

"I could have, but my phone died so I decided to just show up and see what happens" he shrugged.

"Ok" I shrug "Let's go."

He opened the door for me and then got in.

We were quiet the whole ride to my house. I didn't want to be the one to break the silence, so I didn't. He didn't either.

It was strange really. He shows up to pick me up after
school with a smooth scenario and now he's quiet. He has
to have something to say. When we pull up, he's still quiet.
He turned the car off, got out of the car and came around to
let me out of the car too.

"So, you really just wanted to take me home? You
didn't want to talk about anything? You don't have
anything to say to me?"

"Well," he shrugged, "do you have anything to say
to me?"

"Thanks for the ride", I shrug, and I go into the
house. *Does he know he's missing his mark?* Before I could
think my next thought, he knocked on the door. I opened it
and he said,

"You just gon' leave me out here though?"

"Oh, my bad".

"You do know that I wanted to bring you home for
a reason, right?"

"Well, I thought so at first, but we were silent the
whole way here so now I really don't know." I gave him a
look of indifference.

"I wanted to ask you something about homeboy, but
I figured that conversation was off limits."

"I can see why you think that but no. He's not off
limits. He's just my homeboy. I was encouraging him to
talk to this girl who was obviously into him." Most of what
I said was true.

"Ok" he said with a thoughtful look on his face.

"What?" I ask. I could tell that he knew that Mike
was some kind of competition for him.

"I was just wondering if you were going to leave me
out here or invite me in."

"Well, I had originally planned to leave you out
there, but I guess you can come in."

"It's the face, isn't it?" he smiled and rubbed his chin. Of course it's the face but I most certainly will not let him know that. His head is big enough.

"No, it just seems like the right thing to do since we're having a conversation and all." I open the door wider for him to come in, but I don't step aside. He steps right up to me. My body heats a little and I step aside and take a deep breath to settle myself. It doesn't work so I do it again. Still not settled. *Why is he having this effect on me?* I am not cooling off. I'm only heating up more. *What is wrong with me?* He finally takes another step to pass by and lightly brushes my shoulder. I shiver a little on the inside.

"You good?" he asks, "you look a little flustered."

"Huh? Yeah, I, uh, I'm uh, I'm good." I can barely get the words out.

"Why are you still standing by the door? Come chill with me for a minute."
I close the door and sit on the sofa next to him suddenly feeling a little uncomfortable, so I move to the chair.

"So, what's up Lorde?" Just as I'm about to answer my parents walk through the door. "Hey mom. Hi daddy" I greet them as they come through the door. "Hey baby girl" my dad says.

"Hey baby Lorde. It's report card day. Let's see it" my mom requests with a smile.

"There must be something wrong. She's not up waving it in our faces."

"Nah there's nothing wrong" my mother says noticing the boy in the living room.

"Dr. Alexander", Brian says stepping forward and extending his hand for him to shake. My dad likes Brian so of course he took his hand and shook it. "Mrs. Alexander it's"

"Dr. Alexander" my father corrected him before anyone else, especially my mother, could.

"Excuse me" he cleared his throat, "Dr. Alexander it's a pleasure to finally meet you. Please forgive me I was unaware that you too are a doctor. What kind of medicine do you practice?" My mother is impressed. I can tell.

"I am a general surgeon".

"This is Brian Dixon my dad says to my mother "remember the student I was telling you about?"

"Oh yes she says so you're interested in plastics. I can see that. You're pretty enough" she said. We all laughed. I slipped away while they talked to Brian. I returned with my report card.

"That's my baby girl. She's an absolute genius" my dad said.

"Let's go out and celebrate your genius." "I'm sorry Brian did I ask you to meet me here for something?"

"Uh no sir" he answered. "I gave Lorde a ride home from school."

"I see" he said. "Would you like to join us this evening?" Brian looked at me and then back to my father.

"No thank you sir. Thanks for the invite but I was just leaving." I look at him and frown. "Thanks for the ride" I say with attitude. "Anytime" he says. My parents go upstairs as he turns to the door. I follow him to the door and open it.

"What's up?" He turns and ask.

"You should come with us to dinner."

"I think we should get to know each other a little bit before we start having family dinners."

"Well word to the wise. There's no way around it if you want to date me. You're going to have to get through a family dinner eventually."

"Really? I didn't take your parents for the strict type".

"They're not strict. They just care. I make my own decisions while allowing them to care. Sometimes they agree with my decisions and sometimes they don't but at least they're a part of them. My parents are actually pretty amazing" I whisper.

"Well, you said you want to get to know me to determine if you wanted to go on date with me. I want to get to know you before I participate in family dinner. And anyway, family dinner is a type of a date. I'm going to be under a microscope."

"Well, my dad already knows plenty about you already, doesn't he?"

"Well yeah. He is my mentor."

"Well," I roll my eyes "just because he likes you" I pointed to my dad "doesn't mean that I forgive you," I pointed to myself.

"Come on Lorde".

"No don't come on Lorde me. You know how I feel about lying. What is my dad talking about? There you go again. You didn't have a reason to lie to me."

"I graduate next year and you're upset with me for securing my future? What did you think my business was with your dad?"

"You didn't have to hide it from me."

"I wasn't hiding anything from you. I just didn't feel the need to tell you when you're not really giving me the time of day."

"You still should have said something. Especially knowing that you were going to be hanging around my house".

"Ok well is there redemption?" He smiled.

"Are we ready?" My mother asked as she came downstairs. I look at Brian.

"Well Mr. Dixon?"

"So will your friend be joining us for dinner this evening?" She looked at me as if she expected me to answer. I look at him to find him looking at me. He was waiting for me to answer his question before I answered my mother. I rolled my eyes and before I could answer he said

"Yes ma'am I will be joining you. Thanks for the invitation.

Chapter 17

When I get to school, I put the word out for Mike to meet me in the auditorium. Any other time I would have just called or sent a text message. I don't want to. I know it will work because…well this is high school. I also learned that everyone is just counting the days for us to announce that we are a couple, which we won't do because we are just friends.

I sit in the front of the auditorium and wait for him to arrive. When he does I get up and hug him and sit back down. I pull him down to the seat next to mine. I take a deep breath

"Good morning" I say

"What's up?" He asks with skepticism written all over his face.

"What's wrong?" he nodded to me

"Nothing" I say unconvincingly even to me.

"Oh, something's up." He left it at that. He didn't press me out. He just sat back in his seat and looked at me.

"Walk with me" I say standing up to leave.

"Now you know I'm walking you to class" he smiles and takes my hand for me to sit back down.

"No. Walk with me." I pull my hand away and pull his forearm for him to get up.

"Walk with you?" his forehead wrinkles.

"Walk with me" I say again with raised eyebrows.

"Walk with you?" he says looking into my eyes for answers to questions he hasn't asked yet.

"Really? I said walk with me boy. What part don't you understand?"
He smiled.

"I don't understand the part where you want to skip class and stay in the school that holds the classes that you're skipping."

"Ha ha ha very funny. I need to talk to you about something. Are you going to walk with me or are you just going to stand there and keep mocking me?"

"I guess I'll walk with you" he said slowly. The bell rings and we leave the auditorium and start walking.

"Wait" he says, "we have to go to our first class".

"Why?"

"Because if we don't then they're going to leave that automated message on our parent's phone."

"What automated message"

"You know, the one that says that you were tardy or didn't come to school". I have no idea what he's talking about.

"Oh, I didn't know about that."

"That's what you got me for. I told you I got you girl."

"I don't care about that message" My parents know I'm at school.

"Yeah, but I do care. Don't worry Goddess, I'll be there waiting for you as soon as class lets out." I had no doubt that he would be.

As much as Mike stressed that we are just friends, I know that he likes me as much more. Even with Katrina shooting her shot. He may be entertaining her right now,

but he doesn't like her like that. As promised Mike is right
outside my classroom door when the bell rings. We begin
to walk, and he stops in front of my next class.

"What are you doing?" I frown.

"I forgot I have a quiz in my next class so we're
going to have to do this after." How convenient he has a
quiz. I know what this is. He's playing games and I'm not
for it. It's cool though. I know how to get what I want.

"Alright" I say looking down at my shoes and then
back up and looked around and sighed.

"Hey" he turned my face to his "I got you. We're
going to talk." I wrap my arms around his neck and whisper

"We don't really have to. I just wanted to tell you
that I can't kiss you anymore".

"What?" he says as I let him go and go into class
just as the bell rings. He's definitely going to want to walk
with me now. Just as I begin to gloat over my success, I get
a text from Brian to meet him outside after class is over. I
get excused from class five minutes early to use the
bathroom. Mr. Saunders didn't want to let me go but even
less he wanted to hear about my woman problems so he
shoo-ed me out of the door. As I walk out of the doors of
the school Brian lifted me from the ground to his lips and
kissed me. It was the perfect kiss. He held me there for a
moment looking me in the eyes and I was impressed that he
could do it. And with no problems. As he put me down, I
reach up and gently grab his arms. I realize that it was the
first time I have touched him like this. I can feel the
muscles he keeps hidden under a hoodie. It is the first time
we kissed like this. I don't know why we kissed. It was a
really good kiss, but I don't know why it happened. When
he left school earlier, I thought he was avoiding me. I guess
I was wrong about that.

"Hey" I say looking up at him. I have to put my
head all the way up to look at him.

"Hey" He says looking into my eyes. I back away from him a little.

"So, what's up? What was so urgent that you needed come back here?"

"Nothing" He smiled. I used to hate that gorgeous smile but now all of a sudden that smile was everything.

"Nothing?" I say raising my eyebrows

"Nothing" he shrugs still smiling.

"I just wanted to see you and kiss you. And properly say goodbye. Enjoy the rest of your day"
He said turning and walking to his car. As I open the door Brian calls out

"Hey Lorde." I turn around.

"You have a ride home or should I be here when school lets out?" I run up to him and kiss him again. I don't know exactly why but I'm sure it had something to do with how the first one made me feel.

"I have a ride"
I turn and run back into the school. As I come in Mike is walking by.

"Hey" I jog to catch up to him.

"Just getting back from standing me up?" He asks sarcastically.

"Yes, and I'm sorry"

"It's cool. So, what's up you ready to walk?"

"The real question is are you ready to walk?"
He hesitates for a moment and says, "probably not".

'Why not?" I ask almost pouting.

"I don't think I want to hear what you want to tell me", He shrugged, "You already said we can't kiss anymore so the reason why is the reason we're walking".
He was right that was the reason we were walking.

"Come on" He said leading the way.

"So how are things with Katrina?" He doesn't answer he just shrugs. We keep walking. "You mad at me or something?"

"Yeah, a little bit'

"For what?"

"Why does it have to be him? It could have been anyone else but him. I told you to be careful and now he's your boyfriend?"

"Well not exactly my boyfriend yet. That's why I need to talk to you." And then out of nowhere he kissed me. A kiss that made my knees buckle.

"This isn't walk with me conversation. We'll talk about it after school. I'll meet you at your locker when it's time to go." I can't move my legs to walk away or chase him. I'm not even sure if I've tried.

"Wait" I say before he can walk away. He turns back to face me.

"Nothing. Never mind. I'll see you after school". I find my legs and turn to walk away, and he calls out

"Goddess" I turn to look at him. He walks up to me. "You know what? This is walk with me conversation."

"I know" I tried to hold back a smile, but I couldn't.

"So, what's up why can't I kiss you anymore?" *Because for some odd reason people think they can just kiss me whenever they feel like it and I think I just want to kiss Brian for now,* I want to say. Instead, I say

"Because it's overwhelming."

"What are you talking about?"

"Not what, who. You, Simone, Brian. It's too much for me right now. At some point all of you got the idea in your head that you can just kiss me whenever you want. It's overwhelming. I don't need to kiss or be kissed for a while."

"Well buckle up buttercup because trust me when I say that we are not the only people competing for your affections." He stopped and thought for a second "Wait. You kissed dude?" his forehead wrinkles

My eyes widen. Out of everything I just said all he heard was that I kissed Brian.

"What do you have against Brian?" I really am curious.

"Do your research Goddess." Mike patted me on top of my head. *Is he serious? Did he really just pat me on the head?*

"See, the problem is you *think* that I don't know who I'm dealing with. The problem is that you don't know who I am. You need to do your research on me because it's you who don't know who it is that you are dealing with".

"Ok" he said backing down. We walked in silence for a moment.

"So why can't we kiss anymore? I'm confused" he broke the silence.

"Because from here on out I'm not kissing anyone I'm not dating."

"Well, I take you out all the time. I should be able to kiss you.

"Yea well we are not dating."

"You need to just stop all these games and be my girl. Or at least confess to being my girl."

"I really hope that's not your way of asking me to be your girlfriend because...hell no."

"Hell no?"

"Did I stutter?" I gave him a look of disgust.

"Are you sure this doesn't have nothing to do with dude? You sure he's not your boyfriend?"

"I think I would know if he was." I didn't tell him that I might want him to be.

"Yeah ok. Your actions and your words are strangers sometimes."

"What do you mean?"

"They don't always meet."

"I could say the same thing about you. You've been saying that we can't date yet and all of a sudden you want to get together." I wait for a response, but I didn't get one. "Let me guess. It's because you aren't really convinced that

Trey is my best friend. Possibly, but for some reason I don't think that's what it is. Oh! you heard about Simone kissing me. No, you're not threatened by *that* because you don't think that you could *possibly* 'lose your girl' to a girl. So that leaves Brian. For whatever reason you are threatened by him and you refuse to lose me to him." I put my hands on my hips. I don't mention Demetri because I haven't seen him lately so I'm guessing he's already won that battle.

"You don't have all of the answers. Like I said, we aren't the only ones competing for your affections. You can't be mad at me for changing my mind about wanting a girlfriend."

"Yes, I can because it will be my heart that gets broken because you decide to change your mind again. I don't have time for your foolishness Mike." When the bell rings I realize that I walked around during my whole lunch period and now I am hungry.

"I'll see you after school" Mike said after giving me another knee-buckling kiss.

"Didn't I say no more kissing?" I try to catch my breath without being too obvious about it.

"Yup" he said as he nudged me into the classroom.

At the end of the day Mike waited for me by the front door of the school. I had planned to take the bus to avoid him. That plan went out the window when I saw him. I needed to talk to him anyway.

"So what's really up?" He asks as I approached the front door. I felt like everyone was staring at us. I take a quick look to my left and my right and people are definitely looking at me.

"Why would you do that?"

"Do what?" He looked confused. I wanted to slap the look off of his face for acting dumb.

"You know what I'm talking about." I'm almost yelling. He takes a quick look around and notices that people are watching us. If it were any other girl, he wouldn't care. He would have it out with her right there. Somehow, he knows that he isn't ready for the embarrassment that I can deliver.

"Come on" he pulls me by the hand.

"What was that?" I ask as soon as we pull out of the school parking lot.

"That was me avoiding a scene."

"What would have avoided a scene would have been to not kiss me in the middle of the hallway where everyone could see. You embarrassed the shit out of me"

"How did I embarrass you?"

"How did you embarrass me? I was avoiding everyone like they were the fucking paparazzi. *Oh my goodness Lorde I didn't know you were dating Mike Sinclair. What's he like'* and *'oh snap Mike snagged the Alexander princess. Tell me, how'd he do it?'* We're not even dating" I snap.

"Well, we can be" he smiled. I don't say anything I just look at him. Not a nasty look just a straight-faced look that I knew he couldn't decipher the meaning of if he tried.

"Look Lorde, you know I like you. You know I've liked you from the beginning."

"From the beginning? How would I have known that from the beginning? Because you tracked me down for my number? You didn't use it so how would I know something like that?" I hear my voice getting louder. "How am I supposed to know that you want to be together? He's silent for a moment before he finally speaks.

"I thought I made it clear that I wanted to be with you. That I wanted to get to know you."

"No" I interrupt him. "You didn't. I thought you liked Lola for a little while there."

"Lola?" he repeated "Lola? Where'd you get that idea?"

"Your grand gesture for her" I shrug.

"What are you talking about?" He looked genuinely confused. He really has no idea what I'm talking about.

"Taking her to meet your aunt? You knew that she idolizes your aunt and you fulfilled one of her life-long dreams." Mike took a moment. I could tell he was beating himself up internally.

"Goddess, I did that because she was always around. I was making room for me to get to know you. I thought it would work, but now I know why it hasn't. You really thought I was into Lola?" He looks like he has a bad taste in his mouth.

"Yeah" I feel a little foolish now. Lola really was always there with us whether I invited her or not. Of course, he was trying to get her out of the way. She never left on her own. I am now realizing that I am part of the problem. I don't set boundaries. That still doesn't excuse him from his part though. He could have said something, and I could have gotten her to go somewhere.

"Look Lorde she's cool and all but before her internship she was always around. I felt like a third wheel. I was trying to get to know you, not build a friendship circle with the three of us."

"And you do that by fulfilling a lifelong dream of the girl you thought to be my absolute best friend? Don't you think that's a little backwards?"

"First of all, we both know that Trey is your absolute best friend."

"You didn't know that." I interrupt him. he ignores me an continues.

"Lola was a close second, but I don't see you two being friends any time soon based off of how y'all area acting. Anyway, don't you think it's a little backwards that you were still kissing me even after the fact? I mean that's if you really did think I was into her."

"No. She has no interest in you. I was doing nothing wrong. You on the other hand may not have realized that you were being a dumbass, but you were."

Chapter 18

"Ok so listen. You gon' be my girl or not? I'm tired of chasing you girl." It is way too early for me to be dealing with Mike and his nonsense right now. It's been three days since I told him we couldn't kiss, and he's made a point to do it every one of them. That hasn't stopped me from kissing Brian though. I like the way he picks me up and squeeze me tight when he kiss me.

"I'm not running so either you're chasing someone else or you're running in circles". I walk away leaving Mike standing in the middle of the hallway. He was really starting to get on my nerves. He jogged and caught up to me.

"That doesn't answer my question"

"Oh? You sure? You should think about it" I was so glad that we were approaching the door to my class. I walked in, again leaving Mike where he was.

I have no idea how I made it through the day. I couldn't concentrate on much of anything at school and when I got home, I couldn't concentrate on my homework either. I was too busy trying to figure out why my life is moving so fast.

~ ~ ~ ~ ~

"Earth to Lorde" Trey said snapping his fingers in my face.

'I'm sorry what did you say?"
Apparently, he had been talking to me the whole time but have no idea about what. I attempt to listen to him to maybe put some of the pieces together, but I was just too distracted by my own thoughts.

"Look. I'm going to leave you with your thoughts." Trey gathered his things to leave.

"Oh no stay I'm sorry I'm listening" I lie.

"No, you're not and it's cool. I'll see you later. Call me if you need to talk". He gave me a reassuring smile. I could tell that he didn't mean what he was saying so I convince him to stay. I thought I was about to be helping him work through an issue. I really wish I would have been listening the first time around or I wouldn't be in the middle of a plan to break up with Chantel. *How do I get myself into these situations?* Next time I'll be sure to avoid words like *anything* when talking to Trey. I know better. I should've been more careful.

After Trey leaves, I still didn't get any work done. I just sat on my bed looking at the ceiling. When I finally sat up I noticed a gift box on my dresser. Where did that come from? Did Trey leave it? Was it there the whole time? I get up to examine the box. There was a small envelope attached with my name on it. I open it up and read the note on the inside. It's from Brian. I smile a little wondering what could be in the box. Instead of opening it I decide to call him. He doesn't pick up and I don't leave a message. I look at the gift again. I can't just open it because opening it would mean that I was interested. I can't like him. I don't want to like him. Actually, I do want to like him, and I can. I'm just a little too confused about my life right now. I decide not to open it. At least not yet. I put the gift back on my dresser. I decide it's time to clear my head and focus.

Maybe some fresh air will do me some good. I decide to go for a walk.

When I returned home from my walk, I feel refreshed and ready to work. It really did help clear my head. Just as I finish my homework Brian calls. I contemplate not answering. I'm sure it's about the gift that I haven't opened yet.

"Hello" I answer

"Hello, how are you?"

"Well, I just finished my homework so I'm feeling pretty accomplished. How are you?"

"Well, I'm curious. Did you get the gift I sent?"

"Yeah, I got it"

"So how do you feel about it?

"Oh, I haven't opened it yet."

"Do you plan to open it?"

"I do I just haven't really had the time until now and I'm talking to you so you can just tell me what it is."

"No, you can open it and find out what it is and call me back."

"What if it's something I don't want?" he doesn't answer. "Ok fine" I sigh.

"And Lorde?" he says before I can hang up

What's up?

"Don't not open it because I told you to please?"

"You're getting to know me pretty well aren't you?"

"Just your pattern of stubbornness."

"Bye Mr. Dixon."

"Oh, we're back to that now?"

"Would you like to go back to Brian?"

"No, I like the progress. I think Mr. Dixon is growing on me."

"Bye Mr. Dixon" I hang up the phone.

I stare at the package for a while. At first I had no intention
on opening it, but now I'm curious. Especially now that he
called about it. I guess it's really because he doesn't care if
I want it or not, it's mine regardless. I'm tempted not to
open it because he told me to and even more because he
told me to call him back after I do. Maybe I'll open it and
not call him until tomorrow. Yeah, I know I'm all over the
place. And yes I do know that my petty is on high right
now.

     "Hey Lorde, who sent you a gift?"
my dad asks interrupting the madness going on in my head.

     "Brian" I answer. His eyebrows raise. I know he
wants to know more but he doesn't ask.

     "Ok well I'll leave you to it" he says.

     "No, no, don't leave me to it. Please stay". I ask
him to stay mainly because I do not need to be left alone
with my thoughts. My dad takes a seat on my bed, but he's
quiet. Now I'm looking at the gift again.

     "You know what? I'm not going to open it right
now. You don't have to stay here" He leaves the room and
closes the door behind him. He thinks I'm going to open it.
I'm not. I'm too tired to think about it right now. I know he
just left but I need to talk to Trey, so I call him back over.
This is much too serious to talk about over the phone.

     "What's up?" Trey asks when he walks into my
room. "Why you and Mike not talking?" He asked before I
could answer the first question.

     "It's not that we're not talking. It's him not talking
to me. What makes you think we're not talking?" This is
not the conversation I called him over to have, and when
did he get to be so buddy buddy with Mike?

     "Well, you didn't come to school together and he
alluded to it when I asked where you were this morning.
You know. When you didn't show up together". He gave
me a knowing look. "He also hasn't been walking you to
class. The last time I saw you together was when you left

him standing outside of your class earlier today". I didn't know he saw that "Yes I saw that" he read my mind. "Oh! and let us not forget that the whole school saw him kiss you that day. And I mean everybody" he waved his hands across the air for dramatic effect. "So, princess, what's up?"

      "Nothing" I say nonchalantly.

      "It was the kiss wasn't it? You didn't want everyone to see it did you?" he gives me a knowing look.

      "No, I didn't. It embarrassed the shit out of me." I felt myself getting upset and took a deep breath. "That's not why I called you over though. I don't want to talk about Mike. I want to talk about Brian.

      "You talking about dude across the street that's always hanging around? What about him". I fill him in on what's been going on with Brian and me. I like talking to Trey because he always helps me to keep my focus and how to get out of my own way. I know that I don't want a boyfriend. I know that this is all new and I'm just having my fun. There's nothing wrong with me choosing to not be in a relationship that I'm not ready for. Liking someone is confusing enough anyway. I ask Trey if I should open the gift and he didn't understand why I was stalling. I love surprises. I love gifts. I guess I haven't opened it yet because I don't know what it means.

      Trey is talking to me about something but I don't tune in until I hear Mary's name.

      "No Trey. Didn't' you just break up with Chantel? Correction, didn't I just do it for you? Either find another girl or keep TJ in your pants." He tries to convince me that he needs to be with Mary and I remind him of how big our school is trying to convince him that she isn't the one. We decided to agree to disagree and now I possibly have to find a new group of friends.

      "You don't have to find a new group of friends. We are the group of friends that people want in on."

"Don't flatter yourself. There's only two of us".

"Don't downplay yourself. You were pretty big deal before I got back and now that we're back together" he trails off into his own thoughts. I usher him out before he could deliver a monologue on how amazing he is.

"Stalk much?" I say as I let Trey out and Brian in.

"You're funny" he said as he brushed past me. "What's up? Did you catch the bus home today?"

"Why do you ask?

"Well, I haven't seen old boy around here in a minute."

"Yeah", I shrug, "I caught the bus home today."

"Why didn't you call? You know I would've come to get you. I've been trying to fall back and not seem like a creep by just showing up at the school to pick you up." It wouldn't be creepy because he attends the school but I don't say anything. I just shrug again.

"I don't like you catching the bus. Next time call me." He strokes my cheek with his index finger.

"Alright", I shrug nonchalantly.

"Lorde what's wrong?" he frowns.

"Nothing". I shake my head. "Nothing is wrong". He puts his hands on my shoulders and suddenly my insides have awakened and I stand up straight as a fleet of butterflies go from my stomach down to my vagina.

"Something is wrong. I mean it's cool if you're not trying to talk about it."

"I'm really not." I try to ignore the tingling feeling that is threatening to take over my body.

"Well, I'm here if you do."

"Thanks" I sigh.

"Your pops home?"

"No, he's not here. He was but I think he got called to the hospital. You check there yet?"

"Nah not yet. I'll catch you later" he said bear hugging me. Don't for get to call me when you finally get around to opening that gift."

I have no intention of opening that gift any time soon.

Chapter 19

I keep thinking about Mike and what he said. Could he be serious about wanting to be together? Is it real or is he just trying to get with me so no one else can? After I finish my homework, I decide to give him a call. He answers on the first ring.

"What's up Shorty?" He never calls me that. I don't like it.

"Are you and Katrina a thing?" I decide to get straight to the point.

"No. You know I don't have a girlfriend. Why what's up?"

"Then why is that", I stop and take a deep breath, "why is she always in your face then?"

"Uh because she likes me?" he said like more of a question than an answer. "You said so yourself."

"Ok but why you always entertaining her? You like her or something?" I don't know why I'm giving him so much attitude, but it's too late to back down now.

"You're the one who told me to do my thing remember?" He raises his eyebrows and looks like he doesn't want my drama today. Too late. I woke up and chose drama today. I chose drama and I chose to give it all to Mike Sinclair.

"Whatever" I scoff. "You might as well just start Mike Sinclair entertainment since business is so booming." I snap at him.

"Lorde what? What do you want from me? Do you not want me entertaining her because you don't like *her*, or do you not want me entertaining *anybody*?

"I DON'T WANT YOU ENTERTAINING ANYBODY BUT ME". I hang up on him. Fifteen minutes later he rings my doorbell. He looked relieve that it was me who answered instead of someone else.

"Can we talk?" he asks when I answer the door.

"Yeah", I say stepping out onto the porch. We sit quietly on the porch for a few minutes. We exchange glances and shy smiles. I stick my tongue out at him and he returns the gesture.

"So, what's up?" he put his hand on my thigh. His touch sent a tingling sensation throughout my body and I shift a little in my seat. I take a deep breath, but it doesn't calm me.

"You don't want me to pay attention to anyone but you. You ready to do this?" I don't answer his question. I just look at him. He is asking me to be his girlfriend, but I don't like the way he's doing it.

"Ready to do what?" I roll my eyes. I still have a slight attitude. He picked up on it. I could tell I was frustrating him, but he didn't show it. Instead, he took a deep breath.

"Lorde look at me."
I don't. I just keep looking ahead at nothing in particular. My eyes land on Brian's house and immediately I regret staying on the porch instead of going in the house. Oh well. What's done is done. I'm not going inside.

"Can you please look at me?" I oblige.

"I know that I said I wanted something different with you. I know you said that you want us to be friends and I said that would be enough for me. Well, it's not. I don't even know what that means anymore. Something different for me is what we have but something different is also a relationship. I've never really had one. What we have isn't enough anymore. Not when we keep changing what it means to be friends. I really like you. I want you to be my girlfriend. I want to kiss you and not care who sees. I don't want you kissing other people and I don't want to either. I want us to be public. I don't want to be your little secret anymore. I don't think I can be. Can you handle that? Will you be my girlfriend?"

I have definitely just made a mistake. I *know* I just told him I only want him entertaining me. Did that mean I wanted him to be my boyfriend? What about Brian. I like him. I might want him to be my boyfriend too. And Simone. I know she likes me. I don't know if I like her like that, but let's face it. That girl has the kiss of an angel.

"I don't know if I can handle it, but I can try." My voice barely audible.

"What does that mean?" Mike is being much more patient with me right now than he usually is.

"It means yes. I'll try to be your girlfriend" I look down at my hands. I know he has no idea what that means because I don't even know what it means.

"And I promise not to entertain any girls but you" he says lifting my head by my chin and smiling. I look into his eyes searching to find truth in them and he kisses me. A heart melting kiss. A kiss that I'm so glad I'm not standing up for. A kiss that made sure that I didn't want to kiss anyone else. I giggle on the inside remembering that he told me that he was going to do it. I guess I had to wait for the right time.

I know there's something more he wants to tell me. I also know that it has something to do with another girl.

He's been doing his thing around school as he normally does so I know there's something I just don't know what it is.

"I have something to tell you."
I knew it. I'm not even surprised.

~ ~ ~ ~ ~

I sit in silence for a moment. It doesn't last long because Mike breaks it.

"What's up what's on your mind?"

"Are you sure you're ready for this?" I ask him.

"Yeah, I'm sure. Are you sure?""

"Not at all I chuckle. I'm not the girlfriend type any more than you're the boyfriend type."

"Aww" he groans, "now I gotta show you that I'm the boyfriend type" he says in a low growl. I've never heard him growl before and it sends a slight tingle between my thighs.

"No. Just don't embarrass me. You graduate this year. I still have to be here when you're gone"

"I got you he leaned in for a kiss."

"No no no no no" I say putting my hand over his mouth. He gently pulled my hand down. "Lorde, I promise. I'm yours and yours only."

I don't know how to tell him that I'm not worried about being his only. I'm worried that I like him and two other people. I'm worried that if I say something he'll judge me for one of them being a girl or even for liking more than one person at a time especially since I told him not to entertain other girls. I'm worried that I have too many unanswered questions about love and relationships.

"I'm not worried about that" Mike says interrupting my internal freak out.

"Lorde remember when we first met, and you told me to holla at you when I'm ready for change?"

"Yeah, I'm surprised you remember that."
"I do...and this is me being ready for change baby."
"Ok" I shrug. "Change is good" I kiss him.
"Ice cream?" He offers my favorite treat.
"Yes" I smile.
"Cool go and get your shoes on."

I get one shoe on before I start to freak out. It just hit me. I'm officially dating Mike Sinclair. My heart begins to race. I take deep breaths to try to control it. I'm so glad when it finally starts to work. I put on my other shoe and meet Mike back outside.

"Don't think ice-cream is the answer for everything" I say when I return outside. I know I just had a moment, but he doesn't need to know that.

"I know it's not the answer to everything." He smiles. "The good thing", he says kissing me, "is that I know when it *is* the answer."

~ ~ ~ ~ ~

"You real quiet right now. What's on your mind?" Mike asks as we find a table by the window in the ice-cream parlor.

"Us dating. Do you really think it's a good idea?"
"Do you like me?" he asks raising his eyebrows
"Yeah" I smile.

"Good because it's too late. You're already my girl."

"Yeah, but you're leaving before the end of summer." He looks at me with a face of confusion.

"You're worried about breaking up already and we've only been together for like an hour. Chill out". He takes my hand. "The only thing you need to worry about right now is enjoying your ice-cream and figuring out what you're wearing to the prom."

"The prom?"

"Yeah, the prom".

"Oh, I'm not going to prom."

"What you mean you're not going to prom? You're my girlfriend. You're going to be my date." He looked at me as if this was something I should have known. I don't say anything I just slowly shake my head no.

"It's my senior year. I'm not missing my prom." He looks at me as if to say he's going with or without me.

"I'm not asking you to" I shrug.

"So, you want me to take someone else?" I looks at me with suspicion.

"I didn't say that, but I guess I can't really be mad if you did. I mean" I shrug "It is your prom"

"Stop playing with me girl you going to prom with me."

"No, I'm not" I chuckled.

"But you have to" he pleaded

"Why do I have to?"

"Why wouldn't you want to?"

"Because, I already have plans. I'm supposed to visit my grandparents that weekend."

"You're going to choose going to your grandparents house over going to the prom with me?"

"Uh" I put my hand up "my grandparents are great." I roll my eyes. "I'll think about it" I shrug.

"You'll think about it? Seriously?"

"Yeah seriously. I take this trip every year and they're looking forward to seeing me."

"Alright" he sighed.

"Don't be mad at me. I'll make it up to you."

"Yeah? How are you going to do that? He smiled mischievously. I move to sit next to him and kiss him on the cheek.

"I don't know yet" I kiss his cheek again. "Let's talk about this another time" I say. "Like you said. We've only been together for like an hour" I smile.

"You drive me crazy" Mike says. "Are you going to always be this difficult?"

"Difficult?"

"Yes difficult". He raised his eyebrows.

"I asked you if you were sure you wanted to do this." I wave my hands down my body.

"True. You can't keep playing hard to get when I already have you though."

"If you say so" I wink at him.

Chapter 20

"Dad what do you think of grand gestures?"

"I think they're great. They're fun and exciting."

"Ok, but I'm not talking about you dad" I laugh.

"Ok, so what do you want to know?"

"I don't know" I shrug. "What do they mean?

"I think that when someone does a grand gesture, they're trying to tell you something."

"Like what?"

He looks at me like he knows I know the answer. He answers anyway. I'm glad he does because I don't know the answer.

"Well, it depends on who it is. It's usually someone trying to tell you that they like you or show you how much they like you." That sounds accurate to me.

"Ok, but what if they do something for someone else, but for my benefit?"

"Then you must ask yourself if they really did it for you or, are they really into this someone else? Both are possibilities but which do you think is more likely?"
I know which one it is. I just want to know where *my* grand gesture is that benefits *me*.

"What's this about baby girl?"

"Mike. He came up with all of these great ways to ask me to prom, but he was never around for me to actually answer until today. He asked me again, but it wasn't in a grand gesture."

"What do you mean he wasn't around for you to answer? You can't ask someone to prom if you aren't in front of them, right?" It was clear by the look on my father's face that he did not like where this was going.

"That's what I thought".

I continued letting him know how Mike had accomplished the impossible and everything else that led me to say yes to going to prom. After listening to the whole story, he says Lorde, I don't really know what to make of all of that but I can say that what I just saw from him seemed to be a grand gesture. It's not every day you get sung to by a boy just for a date to prom. In my day we asked and hoped for a yes. That boy still has to come back and clean up the mess he made in the yard."

"Yeah, but he introduced Lola to her ido,l and it led to the job of her dreams."

My father is looking at me like he has no idea what I'm talking about and is slightly afraid to ask questions.

"Mike and I just started dating." I blurt out. My dad looks at the gift on my dresser.

"You still haven't opened it huh?" He asks tapping on it and completely ignoring what I just said.

"You know something? I've never known anyone to have a gift this long and not open it. Or at least be curious about what's inside. Especially not you."

"Dad I can't" My face begs him not to continue this conversation. He ignores it.

"Why not baby girl?" he raises his eyebrows.

"Because I know it's something great. I know it's something I want and I'm just not ready yet."

He sits quietly for moment just nodding his head.

"It sounds to me like you're afraid that it's a grand gesture from someone who isn't your boyfriend." He's right. I haven't gotten a grand gesture from Mike, so I didn't feel right accepting one from Brian. Even if Brian gave it to me before I started actually dating Mike. Everyone close to me knows that gifts are grand gestures to me.

"Ok whatever I'll open it" I say mainly to myself. I take a deep breath and I open it. I know immediately why he said it was mine regardless. When I open the box at first all I see are glow sticks. I pick up the glow in the dark toys and underneath are two tickets to see my favorite band in concert lying on top of a jean jacket with the band name spray painted on. I look up at my dad and he's still looking at what's in the box. He finally looks up at me. He places his hand on my shoulder and quietly says "Looks like someone's trying to ask you out. I'll leave you to it". As soon as my dad closes the door behind him, I pick up the phone to call Brian.

"So, what do you think? He asks as soon as he picks up the phone.

"I…I…I…Thank you I sigh. I have so many words but none of them come out of my mouth. I just sigh. It's all I can do.

"For the first time in your life, Lorde Alexander, you are speechless." He's right. I am speechless. In fact, I'm so speechless that I can't even comment on his sarcasm. Instead of responding to any of it I change the subject.

"So, what was up with you kissing me?"

"Why you ask that? That was a while ago. And you liked it. And I've done it again since then."

"That's not the point." I say.

"Ok then the point must be that when I turned to leave you decided you liked it so much that you ran up and kissed me again". I don't answer. "Or that you double back every time". I still don't answer. "Is it cool if I come by?"

"No. I don't think that's a very good idea."

"I get it. Your space is your space. I can respect that."

"Yeah, right since when?"

"Ok then don't go anywhere. I'm on my way over."

"Go where? You live across the street?"

~ ~ ~ ~ ~

"I see you've been spending a lot of time with old boy, haven't you?" Brian wasted no time jumping into conversation without greeting me first.

"Yeah so?"

"That's your man now?" I smile at the question.

"Yeah. What? You jealous?"

"A little bit."

"Really?"

"Yeah, I mean I didn't think I would be, but I guess I am."

"I didn't know you liked me like that" I lied.

"Yes you did. It's cool though. Just be careful with dude."

I'm good. I can take care of myself."

"I know you can."

"What's that supposed to mean?"

"You know what it means. It's time for me to fall back."

"What's that supposed to mean?"

"It means it's time for me to go". He stands up and shove his hands in his pockets.

"No! You're not leaving." I wrinkle my forehead.

"Yes I am. Lorde you know that I like you. I'm not about to let you string me along. I'm not a puppet." He turns to leave but turns back. "Do you really think it's

going to work out with Mike? He's never around. I'm
always here. Trey might as well live here."

"Trey what?" Trey walks up to the porch. "Hey,
what's up? He shakes hands with Brian, and I stand and for
a hug.

"Your girl here is dating Mike Sinclair now" Brian
barks

"I know." Trey shrugs "What? You don't like
him?" Brian shoots Trey a look

"You know about this? Why didn't you say
anything? You knew I was trying to get at her" his voice
gets pitchy.

"Yeah, you and every other dude I know. May the
odds be in your favor bruh." Trey shrugged. Brian turned
his attention to me.

"Lorde I'm here more than your man. I call you
whenever I feel like it. I show up here whenever I feel like
it. Trey pulls up unannounced."

"So what?" I wrinkle my forehead

"So pretty soon he's going to start saying something
about it."

"No, he's not."

"Lorde, I did climb through your bedroom window
while you two were making out yesterday. He looked pretty
pissed. You don't think he's going to say something
eventually?" Trey pointed out. I haven't given it that much
thought.

"No, he'll get used to it." I say with an attitude.

"No he won't" Brian chuckled. "I wouldn't if it
were me."

"Well good thing it's not you then." I must of struck
a nerve because Brian left. Just as he got to the middle of
the street, I called him

"Mr. Dixon!". He turned around. "We're on for the
concert, right?" It only seemed right to go with him since
he did buy the tickets. Even if he is being an ass right now.

"Nah take someone else". He turned and continued home.

"Damn girl you were kind of rude to him don't you think?" Trey said with his eyes glued to his phone

"He'll be alright after the concert".

"He just said he's not going" his eyes still on his phone.

"Yes, he is." I already know he's going to go with me. I just have to give him time to cool off.

"As fun as it is walking into all of your drama I came here because there's something I need tell you." Trey finally looks up and he looks serious.

"What's up?" I ask as prompted. I'm a little scared at what he's about to say so I brace myself to hear pretty much anything and hear him out.

"Love is overrated" he said as if he was making an announcement.

"Which girl hurt your feelings"

"You didn't tell me there was some stupid girl code".

"Because you're not a girl" Trey looked enlightened by that statement.

"Facts. I am not a girl. I just like them way too much."

"Love is overrated" I mocked his announcement. I don't know how else to respond to whatever it is he's going through.

"You're probably right. One of the great reasons I don't do girlfriends. I'm surprised you're in a relationship. You're not exactly the girlfriend type." Oh no he's not trying to drag me into his nonsense.

"Why do you say that?" I know my reasons for thinking *that* but I want to hear his.

"Well, that kiss with Brian was pretty intense from the way you described it to me and almost like the next day

you have a boyfriend. Is that good girlfriend behavior?"
He's right but I'm not going to let him know that.

"Yes. I was not dating Mike yet."

"Yeah, but you wanted to be, and it happened the
day after and if you hadn't just told Brian about him being
your dude a few moments ago he probably would have
done it again. He still might I don't know how much he
cares yet." He's right. He has valid reason to believe that
I'm not good girlfriend material. At least not what my
understanding of it is.

"What's really up? Why are you with dude? You
know he's not a good first boyfriend."

"What do you mean? He's cute. He's popular"

"Your first boyfriend is supposed to be a good
experience for you. It's supposed to be special."

"I didn't want to date him per se, but it kind of just
happened."

"How?"

"Well between always being together and the
constant kissing I got curious about dating."

"You're not curious about dating. You're curious
about sex. He keeps going down on you and now you're
curious about sex."

"Well, that was the plan but I don't know now."

"Wait what was the plan?"

"Sex." I look at him like he needs to keep up

"Your plan was sex, and you chose him? Why? Just
because you're curious about sex doesn't mean that you
choose someone and do it."

"Actually, that's exactly how it goes" I chuckle.
"That wasn't my exact plan though Trey. I'm not even sure
it's him I want to do it with.

"Why? You over him already?" I disregard his
smart-ass question.

"I just thought that I would feel different. I mean I
don't feel like a girlfriend."

"Do you get butterflies in your stomach when you see him?"

"Yes" I smile. I have them now and we're just talking about him. I don't tell him that Mike isn't the only one giving me butterflies though. I'm not ready to yet

"Do you smile when you think about him and when you see him?"

"Yes." Again, Mike is not the only one making me smile.

"And that's not a different feeling for you?"

"Well yeah." I don't elaborate. I just leave my answer lingering in the air.

"Then there it is. You feel different." Trey said.

"You get on my nerves" I punch his arm

"I'm just looking out for you. You know what I think?"

"What do you think?" I ask unsure if I want to know.

"I think that you're making a mistake. I don't think you should date dude.".

"Too late now. I've already been dating him". Trey is probably right but I am not trying to hear his logic. He doesn't know any more about relationships than I do. I'll have to figure this out on my own.

Chapter 21

It's here. It's finally here. My birthday is finally here, and it is party day. My hair and nails are already done so I don't have to spend my whole day getting ready. I already have my outfit. I can use this time to stress about no one showing up.

"What's up girl? You nervous about your party tonight?" Trey said plopping down on my bed.

"A little bit. No not really. You coming to my party, right?"

"Now you know I'm coming to your party. That shouldn't even be a question" he lightly smacked my leg.

"Why not? You got things to do remember?"

"Not before I get up on some of them girls that's gon be at your party. It's going to be so lit."

Trey was right I didn't have anything to worry about. My party is live. I was so nervous about the turnout that I could not have imagined the amount of fun I am having. My parents were right to not let me have this party at our house. I'm having so much fun that I don't even notice that Mike has not shown up yet.

"Where is your dude? Girl, stop tryna dance with me." Trey joked when I tapped him on the shoulder.

"Boy please I aint tryna dance with you. I'm trying to introduce you to Leah here but if you're not interes-"

"Whoa whoa whoa. It's Leah you say?" he says stepping in between us and taking her hand in his.

"Good luck girl" I say leaving them to their business. Just as I begin to wonder where Mike is, I notice a boy looking at me from across the room. He looks a little familiar. I'm sure he goes to my school. I have no idea who he is, but he is gorgeous. He doesn't move from where he's standing. We lock eyes and he smiles a bright, dimpled smile that lights up the darkened room and almost made me go over and find out who he is, but someone taps me on the shoulder from behind.

"Happy birthday baby. Congratulations" he said looking around. "It's lit up in here" Mike says picking me up kissing me and putting me back down.

"And you late up in here" I snap into focus and slap him on the arm.

"My bad" he said holding his arm.
"You looking good though" he said smiling.

"Thank you" I could feel myself blushing. "But why are you late though?" I was flattered but not enough to forget what's happening.

"I know you wanted me to be the first one here, but I couldn't be."

"I hope you don't think that's good enough. It's not even a reason"

"What do you want me to say?"

"I want you to say where you've been. I haven't seen or heard from you all day. Why are you late?"

"Don't cause a scene. You don't want to draw that kind of attention to yourself."

"You know what Mike, here's a little unwanted attention for you." I walked away and a group of my friends pulled me into their circle to dance. Perfect I thought. Now I can show him how much fun I can have without him. I put my hands up and sway from side to side and the boy that had been watching me from across the room came up and started dancing with me. I welcomed it. I know it'll bother Mike. I put one hand on his waist and one on his shoulder as we swayed in unison. I glance over and catch Mike staring at me. He walks off. I don't follow him. I know he wants me to, but I don't. This is my party. I don't have to cater to him. *I know wanted something big to happen tonight. I sure hope this is not it.*

~ ~ ~ ~ ~

"Come in and dance with me." Mike says stepping out of the party but holding the door open with his foot. I thought I was escaping, not bringing the party with me.

"Oh, I'm sorry. I didn't know you wanted to dance."

"Stop playing with me girl." Mike held his hand out for me to take. I don't take it.

"Aint nobody playin' witchu." I put my hands on my hips.

"Then what do you call what you're doing?"

"I call it being mad at you" I say sarcastically

"Well put your mad on hold for a moment and come dance with me." He took my hand, and I took it back. He kissed me. I gave in to that. He's just so damned good at it.

"Follow me" I say leading him back inside, but not to where the party is.

"Hold up" he stops me in my tracks. "The party's in there."

"Correction. The party is wherever I am. Follow me." I pull at his arm unsuccessfully.

"Wait a minute he says pulling me back. I want to show you something."

"What?"

"Dance with me for one song and I'll show you" he smiles. I don't even try to resist. We go back to the party and we dance for one song before I ask

"So, what do you want to show me?" I smile.

"Come see."

"Just tell me what it is."

"Girl come on" he said pulling me out of the back door.

"I'm still having fun. I'm not ready to leave yet" I protested.

"Good thing that's not what I want to show you" When we made it to the front there was a horse drawn carriage waiting.

"This is why I was late" he said lifting me up into the carriage. We rode around and talked for about 30 minutes. When we got back, I was in a bit of a romantic daze. "You ready to dance now?" he said carrying me back into the building where the party was still in full swing.

"Am I ready to dance? I was born ready to dance" I say jumping out of his arms and making my way to the dance floor.

Who said birthdays were so great? This is not a happy birthday. It started that way but as the night progresses it's getting worse. Can I just skip 15 and go straight to 16? Isn't that supposed to be the sweet year? If this birthday is a reflection of how 15 will go then I will gladly pass because 15 sucks already.

"Hey, can you come and get me?" I whine into my phone

"Aren't you still at your party? What's wrong? Where's Mike?"

"If you come get me, I'll explain everything on the ride."

"Nah I got somebody with me, so you won't be able to."

"Please don't bring anyone with you" I beg

"I'm in the middle of a date Lorde, she'll be with me. I'm around the corner."

"How do you plan a date the same day as my birthday party.

"I came to the party. I got you something for your birthday. I didn't know I was supposed to stay the whole time." I am already standing outside when Brian pulls up. I didn't want to call him, but I couldn't really call anyone else. Everyone else I know attended my party.

"You look stunning. Simply gorgeous", the girl said from the front passenger seat of Brian's car.

"Thanks. It's my birthday" I say dryly.

"Damn girl that's one hell of a birthday dress". She looked me up and down admiring my look. Brian looks at me like he can see through my dress and quickly look away.

"Thanks." I look back at the girl.

"Why are you leaving your party birthday girl?"

"Party is over, due to a brawl."

"A brawl?" Brian chimed in.

"Oh look who finally has words. Yeah a brawl. A few girls showed up uninvited and started a fight with a girl they thought was me. The bouncers pulled me out before anything could happen and when I got the hell out of there, I called the cops and then you for a ride."

"I'm confused. They wanted to fight you for what?"

"Look at her. She is bad as shit Brian, of course they want to fight her" the girl in the front seat said.

"So where is Mike? Brian asked.

"I'm leaving him here!" I snap.

"Why?"

"Because Brian, can you please just take me home? Ok one more question and I will leave you alone."

"What?" I feign exhaustion.

"Where is Trey?

"He left the party early with some girl. I didn't see who she was, but the after party is at his house."

"You just left Mike Sinclair at your birthday party." Brian evaluated the situation.

"Whoa wait a minute!", the girl in the front seat exclaimed. "You are Mike Sinclair's girlfriend?"

"Yeah" I said freaked out that this girl whom I have never seen before knows me.

"Freshman, birthday party brawl, and to top it off Mike Sinclair is your man. You are a bad bitch".

"Uh thanks. I guess. But Mike is not the reason that I'm the shit. " *Who is this bitch? Who does she think she is?* I saw Brian reach over and touch her leg.

"I'm just Ouch!" she screeched stop squeezing my leg.

"Chill" he said "she's telling you to chill without being mean."

"Telling me? You mean asking?" She looked back at me.

"No, I mean telling you. Just like I'm telling you this date is over" he said stopping the car. I looked out the window to see where we were. We were stopped in front of a house. "This is your stop" he said to the girl. She got and slammed the door shut.

"Lorde hop up front I ain't no chauffeur." I rolled my eyes and move to the front seat.

"What was that about?" I refer to him dismissing his date.

"Nothing. She was getting on my nerves anyway".

"So, you coming to by Trey's for the after party?" I change the subject.

"You're having an after party? You didn't have enough excitement at the actual party? He chuckled. "Will your man be there?"

"I don't know. I'm not there yet." He looked at me sideways then looked away.

"Well, my date is over so I guess I can swing through".

When I got to my house Trey was waiting outside with a panicked look on his face. As I walk up the porch steps, he says

"I promise this isn't a set up." I look at him to try and decipher the meaning of his facial expression.

"Is this about what happened at my party?

"No. Wait. What happened at your party? I tell him what happened after he left, and he was livid. He told me that Mike wasn't there and warned me that if he showed his face then there would definitely be another brawl. Trey didn't like that fact that Mike stood back and let things happen the way they did without stepping in to prevent it. I calm Trey down and he remembers that he was trying to tell me something.

As I change into my after-party outfit, I think of ways to make Trey pay for the huge mistake he's made. Lola and her new crew somehow got invited. Whatever it's my birthday. My mind then shifts to the fine ass dude I met at my party.

"Damn girl you sure you're wearing that dress down to the party?" Trey came in just as I finished dressing. Eyes wide he looked at me up and down and licked his lips. This is the first time he has ever looked at me the way he is now.

"Yeah, what's wrong?" I say smiling and giving a 360 degree turn to show off my whole look.

"No. Change now. I'll be back in a minute."

"Excuse me? You must be saying that you're going to be back in a minute after you handle that little problem you created at your house. If that's not what you're saying, then baby I look good. I'm wearing this dress, now move out of my way" I say pushing past him out of the room and down the steps. As we head to out to Trey's for the afterparty Mike is stepping up to my porch.

"Hold up I left my keys in your room" Trey said and turned around and went back into the house.

"Hey birthday girl you dropped something." He hands me three small boxes and a bouquet of roses. I don't take any of it.

"Goddess" Mike pleads

"Goodbye Mike. It's over."

I go into the house and leave him outside. Trey sees that I'm flustered. He doesn't ask me what's wrong. Instead, he opens the door to see if Mike is still outside. Although he wanted to punch Mike in the face, he still convinced me to go out there and confront him.

"Go ahead out there and handle your business. Whether you stay with him or break up you still have to handle yours." Trey said.

"Alright but you have to come with me". I pull him out the door with me. Mike is standing there again offering me gifts. I handed them to Trey and he and went back into the house to give us some privacy. So much for him being out here with me. I guess it is best that I handle this myself.

"So, what happened? You just left me." Mike initiated conversation.

"Well first of all you can't tell me you didn't witness that ridiculous brawl started by your little fan club." I snap at him.

"Yeah, I was looking for you, but I couldn't find you."

"Yeah, that's because a couple of your lil girlfriends tried to jump me. Or do you not remember that's why the party ended in the first place."

"My girlfriends?"

"Yeah, your little Mike Sinclair fan club. You weren't looking for me. You didn't even call to see where I went."

"I tried but it just kept going to voicemail. That's why I'm here now to see what's up. You don't look beat up or anything."

"That's because I held my own and got the hell out of there as soon as I could. My boyfriend was nowhere to be found. Where the hell were you? You were supposed to make sure I was out of there and good. But I had to fend for myself. And do you know what I saw when I was leaving?"

"What?"

"NOT MY BOYFRIEND!"

Who said birthdays were so great? This is not a happy birthday. I break up with Mike and tell him that we should just be friends because that's all we ever really were anyway. It was never supposed to come to us dating because I had my doubts from the beginning. I told him it would be best if he left and not go to the after party because I wouldn't be able to enjoy myself if he did. He doesn't agree but he does leave.

Chapter 22

"Happy birthday gorgeous" Demetri greeted me at the door to Trey's house. I'm surprised to see him. I'm thankful that Trey immediately begins to usher unwanted guests out of the party.

"Thanks stranger. Where have you been? I haven't been seeing you around." I can't help but smile. I miss seeing Demetri in class every day.

"That's because I haven't been around" he smiles. "I came back for your birthday. I'm leaving again tomorrow."

I'm flattered. I don't know if he's telling me the truth, but it feels good. This is what I mean when I said that Mike isn't the only one delivering smiles and butterflies. Both of which are in my possession at this very moment. Demetri put one arm around my shoulder and with the other hand he produced a gift box.

"Happy fifteenth birthday gorgeous" he smiles. "Open it tonight after everyone leaves but don't wait until tomorrow."

"Because you want to see me open it."

"Yes" he nods. "I have to go but call me when you're about to open it and I'll be back".

"Ok" I say and walk him out. *Not with you trying to tell me what to do on my birthday.* I don't intend to follow his instructions. I don't know why he think I would.

When I finally get into my party and make my rounds, I notice that the cute boy from my party is here. The lighting is better here so I can really see him now. He is fine as hell. His skin is a deep brown, and he has a golden glow. He has long jet-black hair that is braided and rests neatly on his back. And his eyebrows. Why do guys always have the eyebrows that girls would kill for? It just is not fair. His eyes are a seemingly hazel but not really. Maybe they are hazel. I don't know what that color is called but it's gorgeous. He is gorgeous. And now he's walking up to me

"Hi" he smiles. I don't answer I just smile back. "Lorde, right?" he asks with one raised eyebrow.

"Yeah" I say unable to break away from his gaze. "What's your name?"

"John Ryan" he answers still smiling and still gazing into my eyes. "I've seen you around. I was a little surprised to get an invitation since we don't really talk".

"Well, it seems the guestlist was a little out of my hands but I'm glad you got an invite" I say twirling my hair between my fingers.

"Me too. I can't stay too long. I really just came so I can give you this he said slipping a piece of paper into my hand. I open it to find that it is his phone number. "Try not to lose that. Call me if you want to".

"No thank you John Ryan" I say. "Where's your phone?" he gives me his phone and I put my number in. "I know you won't lose it because it's stored in a safe place. You call me if you want to" I wink at him and smile.

"You know, Lorde is the perfect name for you" he said touching my elbow sending a wave of electricity through my body.

"I try to tell people, but everybody wants to give me a nickname" I shake my head.

"Well, like I said, you're perfect" he smiles. "I gotta go. I'll see you around though he says touching my elbow again.

"Can I get a dance though?" I turn around just as the music changes to a slow song and see Brian holding out his hand for me to take.

Before I could answer someone taps me on the shoulder from behind. I take a deep breath and turn to see who it is. It's Simone. I instantly think about the kiss and get excited that she's here. I've been wanting to talk to her, but I haven't had the words. I still don't yet for some reason I'm happy to see her.

"Happy birthday" she says smiling. I let go of Brian's hand and turn and face Simone completely.

"Thank you" I return her smile. She steps closer and gently kiss me and quickly step back.

"I don't like you ignoring me" she said. "Usually, I would just take the hint and move on with my life, but when I kissed you, you kissed me back." I thought she was done but she continued. "I get it. You don't know what to say to me but don't leave me hanging like that again. I don't like that. I'm going to let you think a little bit more before I call you again." She stops to stare at me for a moment and continues again. "You should have something to say by then" she said kissing me and turning to walk away. I grab her hand. She turns back and look me up and down flirtatiously. I'm shocked but amused by her speech.

"Wait a minute" I say still smiling. "You think you can just fuss at me on my birthday and roll out? It don't work like that" I gently pull her in closer and we start dancing. I want to kiss her, but I panic and start to dance the bump instead. *The bump? Who am I my mother?* I'm so relieved when she joins in.

"I wasn't fussing" she giggles.

"It sure seemed like you were fussing to me". I don't know why I can't stop smiling. I know I look like a dork. She's not saying anything so maybe not.

"Did I remember to say happy birthday?" she said and we both giggled. We danced and talked for another two songs.

"So, what was that about?" Brian asked reminding me that he was here. *Oh shit I forgot he was here. And that we were talking. Or about to dance. Or something.* I don't quite remember what was happening before Simone showed up, but it was something. Is it possible that the kiss was so good that I forgot he was here? I'm not even sure Simone was aware that Brian was right there. If she was aware, she most certainly did not care. *Has he been right here the whole time, or did he just come back when we finished dancing?*

Just as the party was ending Mike reappeared. "Need a cleanup crew?"

"You know we do" I say handing him a trash bag as I handed out party favors to my departing guests.

"I take it this was the place to be tonight. You know you're the first to throw a party that everyone was willing to break curfew for?"

"Yeah, I figured. Parties are usually over by midnight". We continue cleaning up in silence. I should tell him to leave because Trey isn't exactly feeling him right now, but I don't. I don't know why. I just don't.

"What's up why you mad at me?" He stops cleaning and stands to look at me.

"I'm not mad at you." I say not looking at him but smiling and thanking my guests for coming.

"Yeah alright. What's up?" He walks closer to me.

"I don't know" I shrug my shoulders. I feel a little awkward seeing and talking to him hours after we broke up. I know we said we could be friends, but I didn't think it would start tonight. I mean I need a day or two. A week maybe. But hours? It's just a little too soon for me. Okay, a lot too soon.

"Yes, you do."

"I'm mad you left."

"No, you're not. You told me to leave, and you meant it "

"You're right. I'm mad you came back. It's too soon." Trey comes over to make sure everything is alright.

"Well damn. I guess I'll see you around. You sure you don't want me to stay and help? Nah I'm staying here tonight. And I have Chantel, Mary and Brianna staying the night here with me. We'll be fine. He looks at Trey and back at me.

"I'll call you tomorrow. One last date?"

"Yeah, I'd like that." He kissed me and I walked him to the door.

"You ok girl? Briana asked me when I walked back into the house. They all saw what happened because they were all eavesdropping.

"Yeah, I'm alright." I fix my posture.

"You know you can talk to us." Chantel said "We're here for you. Heartbreak can be a bitch."

"Yeah" Mary chimed in "We're your girls. We'll help you through it. It's what friends are for."

"I'm not really heartbroken." I say finally sitting down for what feels like the first time tonight.

"Really? Yeah. I mean I'm sad it ended but I'm not heartbroken."

"Ok then" Mary shrugs "what was that with you and Simone?"

When she asks that question I go into a panic. *First of all that bitch is fine as fuck.* Nah I can't say that. To Trey I can, but not to them. I couldn't help but wonder if they would judge me. They keep telling me that we're friends but the only person who has ever really been one to me is Trey. I look at him. He gives me a look that only I understand. Instead of answering the question I change the subject.

"What's up with Briana and Steve though? Y'all danced together all night didn't you? Briana blushed.

"Oh, so is that bae now or what?' Chantel asked. I could sense the hate in her voice, but I didn't say anything. I wonder if anyone else picked up on it.

"Yeah, that's bae" she said still blushing. We all giggled. As we lounge around talking and laughing I thank Trey for throwing my afterparty. Especially since it saved my actual party.

"If you really wanted to thank me, you would've made sure I got one of those goodie bags."

"You mean one of these? I say handing him a bag."

"See that's why you my girl" he kissed me on the forehead. He looked in his bag and then back at me. "This not the bag everybody else got."

"Yes, it is. You just got a little something extra."

"I love you girl" he rumbled, grabbing my face and giving me a big kiss on the forehead.

"I get it" Briana chuckled. "You mean love like that."

"Love like what?" Trey said looking back and forth from Briana to me.

"Nothing" I say giving her an evil look.

"Whatever" she rolled her eyes. Yall need to stop playing anyway."

"Who are you talking about?" I ask genuinely confused about what she is talking about.

"Yaaaaaallll" she said sarcastically pointing back and forth from me to Trey.

"Look Briana, what's between me and Lorde is between me and Lorde. Just because you don't know what's up doesn't mean we don't."

"Well, would either of you care to enlighten me?"

"Not really", he said looking at me. Briana looked at me shaking my head no.

"Oh see that's messed up. We all supposed to be friends."

"No, you're Lorde's friends" he points at each of them. "You've just been getting on my nerves for the last few months."

"Yeah, and what does that make you?" Chantel chimes in.

"Her best and first friend. Her person."

"Then why hasn't she told you about Mike yet?"

I can tell that he is about two seconds away from putting one or all of them out of his house. I want to let it happen because it would be funny to watch but instead, I interrupt their little exchange. I don't need my night to end on a bad note. They make up and we move on.

"It's cool Bri Bri. We are not the same, but guess what? You still my boo girl" he said kissing her cheek.

"Oh I'm good on being your boo. I see where that got Leah tonight" she chuckled."

"Wait what happened with Leah?" Chantel asks with a hint of jealousy in her tone. Even though they're not together anymore, I didn't want to tell her that I hooked Trey up with Leah tonight.

"Oh you didn't notice homegirl left early tonight? Mary put her two cents in. *Where did I find these girls?*

"I guess not" I shrug. I know better than to ask him what happened in front of them, but I couldn't help myself.

"What happened Trey?"

"Nothing" he gives me a look.

"Nope tell her what happened" Mary instigates.

"There's nothing to tell. Your girl just isn't my type" Trey waves her off.

"Since when is hoe not your type?" Chantel snaps. Everyone stops and look at her. "What" she says. I guess she doesn't realize that she just called herself a hoe and I will not be the one to tell her. Apparently no one else wants to be either because no one says anything. We all just look at her.

"Wait, when *is* hoe not your type?" I take the attention off of Chantel and put it back on Trey." I practically gift wrapped a piece of ass for you, and you send her home alone?"

"You did what?" Chantel looked at me.

"Excuse me girls I'm going to have to see you three tomorrow. I need to talk to my best friend. Thanks for coming to the party" I say. Trey gets up on queue in true best friend fashion to lead them to the door. "I'll call you tomorrow" I say as he opens it inviting them to leave. None of them move an inch.

"Girl please. I'm not going home this late. Not after my parents already think I'm staying with you." Chantel speaks first and the other girls agree.

"She was just too ready" Trey said rubbing his head.

"Yeah dummy, that's because her parents are gone for the weekend and left her and her brother home alone" I slapped his shoulder.

"Damn you messed that one up" Mary laughed.

"You could've been getting head and fed all weekend". I looked at Chantel again with raised eyebrows. "What" she shrugs.

"Nothing" I say shaking my head. *Is It possible that she doesn't hear herself when she talks?*

"Let me guess?" Briana says "You don't do that. You're too good for that right?" *Why am I friends with this girl?* "What do you be over here doing? "

"Bri please. Have you met my day one?" I motion toward Trey, "I don't have to do that. I'm the one getting head and fed." I giver her a face that says 'duh'.

"How when Mike's the one coming over?" she plops down on the couch.

"Yeah, to give me head and bring me food." After an extra second I add "Or take me to get food" I giver a side eye.

"So you mean to tell me that you've never given head?" Chantel asks.

"That's exactly what I'm telling you." All three girls look at me like I've grown an extra head.

"How are you getting it without giving it?" Mary asks.

"Me giving it has never even been a part of the conversation but that's not what we're talking about. Trey sir?" I attempt to put the attention back on to him. He's been texting since the attention shifted off of him. I know he hears me trying to get his attention. He's ignoring me and continues texting.

"Trey I know you hear me."

"What do you want Lorde?"

"Why did you send Leah home?"

Before he can answer Trey's mom comes downstairs. We know immediately that we are officially too loud. She gives us the option to quiet down or go home and threatens to send us all home if she has to say anything else.

Chapter 23

"Hey girl you ready?" Simone asked bursting into my room. We've been hanging out a lot since my party. She hasn't stopped randomly kissing me and I don't really know, but I think I'm ok with that.

"Knock much?" Mary rolled her eyes. I don't know why but Mary can't stand Simone.

"Oh hey Mary you coming too?" Simone asked sarcastically

"Nah I'll see you later Lorde". She hopped up to her feet.

"Alright girl I'll call you later" I say as she leaves. Mary absolutely hates Simone. She leaves every time Simone comes around.

"Ready to go where?" I ask Simone.

"Nowhere I just wanted Mary to leave."

"Excuse me?" I ask with raised eyebrows, She chuckles, I frown.

"What?" She's still laughing.

"You can follow her out."

"Are you serious?"

"Dead ass. Bye." I walk to the open door and put my hand on the knob.

"Alright girl damn I guess I'll try again later" she walks toward me and stop in front of me.

"Please don't."

"Damn girl, I thought we were friends."

"Not if you taking the place of my other friends." She's standing directly in front of me and I can feel her breath on my ear.

"I may not like them hoes but I'm not trying to take their spots" she licked her lips and looked me up and down. I blush a little. I know because I can feel the blood rush to my cheeks.

"I know exactly which spot you want and you not getting that either." I wink at her. Now it's her turn to blush.

"Here you go again with that. Lorde you've already made it clear that you aren't interested in me like that." *Wait what? Did I make that clear? I'm not even clear on it how could she be?* I lightly push her back and move to sit in a chair.

"So where are we going?" I say trying to disregard her statement. I don't really know how to respond. What do I say? *No Simone I do like you like that but I don't want to be in a relationship right now?* What does that even mean? Or maybe I should say *I don't want you to be my girlfriend but I do want to keep kissing you but I don't want you to kiss any other girls because then I might want to punch you and them in the face.* That doesn't sound any better. I don't know if I'm a lesbian or not, but I can say that this shit is hard.

"I came to hang out with you. Where do you want to go?" I think for a moment but I don't come up with anything. I remember that I was putting her out, but I've already changed my mind. After I'm quiet for too long she breaks the silence.

"Good because I'd rather do this anyway" she leans down balancing herself on the arms of my chair and kisses me. Heat begins to radiate between my thighs, and I squirm in my seat. She continues to kiss me. After another moment she straddles me and sit on my lap. I panic and stand up. She falls to the floor but jumps right up.

"I'll call you later" she kisses my cheek and leave. *That could have ended better.*

After Simone leaves, I pick up a book with plans to do nothing else with my day but read. I call Trey first to see what he is up to but he doesn't answer. Back to my book plan. Those plans are quickly disrupted when Mike calls. I haven't seen him since my birthday. We still talk from time to time but not too much. I still owe him a date but I didn't think he'd be collecting so soon. He left for college earlier this summer and I didn't expect for him to show up for a while.

"Hello" I answer.

"I'm back. You mind if I slide through right quick?" he says without greeting me.

"Now's not a good time. I'm headed out." In that very moment I decided to go to Trey's instead of waiting for him to call me back. I send him a text while Mike is trying to convince me to wait for him.

"Come on Goddess I won't stay long. I just want to give you something."

"Can we do this later? I gotta go".

"Yeah I guess that's cool."

"Aiight. I'll call you later". I hung up and called Trey.

"I just got your text girl dang" he answered.

"You home?"

"Yeah. Why?"

"I'm on my way."

"MIKE. IS. BACK. AND. HE. WANTS. TO. SEE. ME." I shout as I walk into Trey's room.

"Lorde girl stop making all of that noise in my house" Trey's mom calls up to me.

"Yes ma'am" I call back down the stairs. I know
she hates when I do that, but she would have started fussing
if I didn't answer her and I am not ready for that drama.

"Ok so? You knew he would want to see you when
he got back. You said you were still friends. What's the
problem?" Trey said as I climb in his bed and get under the
blanket.

"I'm nervous. I haven't seen him since my party."

"I thought you were going to see him off" Chantel
says. I didn't notice she was there before she said
something. I look at her and back at Trey.

"Yeah, that didn't happen and now he's back and he
wants to see me."

"Is that why you're dressed for a date?" She must
have noticed my outfit before I climbed in bed.

"You want him to think you're out with someone
else."

"Yeah." Chantel is my friend, but I did not come
here to talk to her.

"Ok so who's about to pick you up?"

"No offense Chantel but I didn't know you were
here. I came to talk to Trey. I don't really want to talk to
you about this." She says something back but I don't hear it
because I'm too busy checking a text message that just
came through. It's Brian. *Yes. Perfect. He wants to see me.*
I tell him to pick me up from Trey's house.

Just like I planned Mike was waiting on my porch
when we pulled up. I told him what was up on the way to
my house, so we set a date for tomorrow instead. Just as I
was about to let myself out

"Wait, hold up a minute" Brian said. He got out of
the car and came around and opened my door. When I got
out, he kissed me on the cheek and winked at me. "Do your
thing" he said. That wasn't planned but it was perfect. It
didn't hurt that he's cute and Mike doesn't like him.

"Thanks" I said giving him a hug and a kiss on the cheek. "You a real one Mr. Dixon" I stroke his face.

I walk toward my house and I can feel him looking at my butt. I'm a little flattered and a little curious about what Mike would say. I hear the car pull off just as I reach the porch.

"Hi Mike" I say as I walk up the steps.

"Hey Goddess" he picked me up and spun me around. "I missed you girl. How is your summer going?"

"So far so good."

"I see. You look good."

"So do you. I see your summer is going great."

"It's my last one here so I better make it good right? I bought you something back" he handed me a bag.

"Thank you" I said opening it. We sat outside and talked for a few minutes and he left. I thought I was going into the house, but Demetri pops up. I haven't seen him since school let out for the summer. He hasn't been around much. We sit outside and talk for a while, but I don't invite him in. I'm waiting for Brian to get back home. I have plans to go across the street and thank him for saving my ass earlier.

Chapter 24

"I thought I wasn't going to see you until tomorrow" Brian opens the door with a surprised look on his face.

"I can leave", I feign a turn.

"Oh nah" he said catching my hand, "now is perfect". He pulled me close and kissed me. He then led me into the house and to the living room.

"I thought you made other plans after you dropped me off". I found a spot on the couch.

"Nothing wrong with chillin' sometimes". He sat down beside me. How was your little visit? I saw your boy. He looked like he was waiting for a while."

"It turned out good." I don't elaborate.

"That's what's up. Not that I'm not happy to see you, but isn't our date supposed to be tomorrow night? Or am I mistaken?"

"No, you're not mistaken. My plans changed." After an awkward silence I lean over and kiss him. We are interrupted by the doorbell.

"Finally, the pizza is here" he said. "You hungry?" he asked as he returns holding the pizza box.

"I'm always hungry" I joke.

This is the first time Brian and I are chilling alone like this and I don't want to ruin it. I don't usually come over when no one is home. It is relaxed but a little intense. It's nice. There's no real pressure. I like it.

We eat pizza, watch tv and cuddle under a blanket. He tickles my knee, but it doesn't tickle. It feels good. The tickle turns into a gentle rub and then a light massage. He rubs up and down my leg again and then does that light massage from my knee to my thigh to the middle of my thighs. I lean over and kiss him but then I pull away. He looks me in the eye as he rubs my leg a little longer then move his hands to the center. I give him a look of both fear and bliss and I'm sure he has no idea what the look actually means. Or maybe he does. He leans over and kiss me as he continues to massage between my legs. I open my legs wider and then get up to straddle him. He keeps his hand where it is the whole time. He doesn't remove it once. He uses the other hand to squeeze my breast over my shirt. Still kissing me it takes a few seconds, but he finds a good rhythm. I feel his penis becoming erect beneath his jeans and I begin to grind slowly. He moves both hands to my waist and assist in my movement. The room is getting hot. Brian removes his shirt, then he removes mine and continue kissing me. I pull away

"When are your parents going to be back?" I can tell by the look on his face that he was not at all worried about his parents until now. He doesn't answer me. He picks me up along with our shirts and carry me up the stairs to his room. He lays me across the bed and take my shoes off. He gets on the bed and kiss simultaneously unbuttoning my pants and crawling his fingers beneath my panties. He doesn't stop kissing me. *How is he so good at this?* He inserts a finger inside of me and suddenly stops. He gets up and with my assistance he removes my jeans. He doesn't remove my panties. Instead, he opens my legs and moves them to the side and lean down and kissed first my inner thigh and then continues to trail kisses from my thighs landing right on top of my center. He looks up at me and slides my panties down. I lift to assist him and before I could lower myself back down there was a finger inside of me as he used the other hand to slip my panties the rest of the way down. I lowered myself slowly and his hand followed at my same pace. When my body finally rests on the bed he climbs up and kiss me deeply never moving his fingers from between my legs. He inserts another finger. I gasp. *Whoa! Ok. Ok. Am I about to let this go further? Are we really going to do this? I'm a virgin. I have to tell him I'm a virgin. Ok. I'm telling him.*

"Are you a virgin? He asked before I could say anything. I am relieved because no words seem to be coming out of my mouth anyway because his fingers are still inside of me. I nod my head yes.

"Are you okay?" I still can't get words out, so I nod again and pull him in for a kiss.

"Are you sure you want to do this? I nod my head again. He stood up and unbuttoned his pants. Just as he was about to take his pants off, he stopped and asked again.

"Are you sure you want to do this? I nod my head yes. "That's not good enough. I need to hear you say it". I give him a confused look. "Consent" he shrugs.

"Good job. Safety then teamwork" I say. "Yes, I'm sure I want to do this." I attempt to pull him down, but he resists. I lie back on the bed. I unsnap my bra and take it off.

"Good girl" he said. I don't know why, but that shit turned me on. If I still had on my panties, they would definitely be wet. Instead, the bed underneath me is damp and getting wetter. He raises up and inserts himself into me and a surge of pain shoots from my opening to my belly button. My eyes widen with shock. Brian sees the look on my face and immediately stops

"Are you ok?" I nod my head up and down

"Yeah" I breath "yeah I'm ok?"

"You want me to stop?" he asks eyebrows raised. I shake my head no. He doesn't move he just looks at me. I take a deep breath

"No." I shake my head again "I don't want you to stop. He slowly begins again. I wince and shake my head yes to signal him to keep going. He does. After a moment the pain turns into pleasure and I'm moving to his rhythm. When it starts to feel really good Brian lets out a long grunting moan and collapses on top of me. *Is that it? Is this what I've been so nervous about? This is what people make a big deal about?* I am so disappointed. He rolls off of me and I quickly jump up and put my clothes back on in a panic.

"Are you alright?" Brian looks at me confused.

"Yeah, I'm good" I say jumping and pulling my pants up and looking around. *I can't believe I just did this. I have to get out of here.*

"Where are you going? Would you like to shower before you go? He asked talking quickly.

"No, I'm good" I say tears forming in my eyes and I'm willing them not to fall, but I fail. He jumps out of the bed and wraps his arms around me.

"It's ok. It's cool. It's ok" he says. He runs to the bathroom. I hear water running and he returns to me and leads me to the bathroom where the bathtub was filling with water and bubbles. He helps me get undressed and into the bathtub and then he disappears. I'm still freaking out, so I take a few deep breaths to try and calm myself. It doesn't work right away but eventually it does and Brian reappears with fresh clothes. I give him a puzzled look.

"I climbed through your window" he says placing my clothes on the toilet. "Are you sure you're ok?" he looks worried.

"Yeah" I say looking at him. He isn't looking at me. He's looking at something on the floor. I follow his gaze and see my blood-stained panties on the floor. My face flushes with embarrassment. I want to jump out of my skin. He kneels over the bathtub and wraps his arms around me. Something about them feel comfortable. No. Safe, but I don't want to be here. I don't want to be in his arms.

"Where have you been young lady?" Trey asked as he entered my bedroom.

"I could ask you the same thing young man" I got up and hugged him.

"Yeah, but I asked you first. You look a little different. Well, not really, but something is definitely different about you" he gives me a look of suspicion.

"Well let me know when you figure it out" I say. He looked at me for another second. I know that look.

"So, where you been?" he says taking a seat at my desk.

Chapter 25

The summer has gone by way too quickly. There's only a
few weeks left of summer vacation then tenth grade here I
come. My life is moving way too fast.

"Hey princess, you good?" Trey asks referring to all
of my lost boyfriends over the summer. I must have drifted
off into thought in the middle of our conversation

Mike didn't last through the school year. Demetri
thinks he can just pop up when he feels like it without
calling. John Ryan calls sporadically and I always miss his
calls, and Brian. Well, I stopped Brian cold turkey after
our…experience.

"Yeah I'm good." He pulls me into him and gives
me the tightest of hugs. "Thank you" I say, still holding on
to him.

"You know I got you. Look on the bright side
though" he says letting me go, "Now we can really turn up.
You've been missing so many parties. I've been needing
you" he says getting excited. Trey and I always go to
parties together.

"First stop, Simone's party tonight" I announce.

"What?" he looks confused.

"We're going to Simone's party" I repeat.

"Simone?" he wrinkles his forehead in confusion.

"Yes Trey, Simone's. I ignore the look he's giving me.

"Simone is going to kiss you as soon as she sees you."

"Good because that's what I want her to do" I look at him.

"You shouldn't lead her on if you not gonna make her your girl."

"Who is the girl here Trey, me or you? *You shouldn't lead her on*" I mock him. "Relax. She's been kissing me all summer and hasn't made me her girl yet either. Nobody is leading anybody on here." I roll my eyes.

As soon as we walk into the party, just as Trey said, Simone walks up to me and kisses me. This time it lasted longer than usual, and I think I felt her squeezing my butt. No. I know she just squeezed my butt.

"Make sure you save me a dance" she whispers in my ear and kisses my cheek.

"Ok" I say looking to my left and seeing Brian with a shocked look on his face. I've been avoiding him since we had sex. I didn't consider that he might be at the party.

"So, you came to a party and accidentally got a girlfriend" Trey teases.

"If she keeps kissing me like that then this is definitely not going to be an accident" I chuckle.

"Lorde are you finally coming out to me?" Trey smiles mischievously

"Coming out? Boy please." I nudge him "I don't even know what I am yet. I know I like kissing both males and Simone. I haven't gotten beyond that so chill."

"I think you should have my player card. You are our new leader. I salute you." Trey turns and salute me.

"I don't know what all that is about, but it's about time you acknowledge my greatness."

We are at the party for about an hour before I decide to find Simone to make good on my promise to dance. I spot Chantel, Mary Brianna by the refreshment table and wave. When Chantel sees me, she waves and looks around. She's looking for Trey. Trey just met some girl named Cheyenne and they're in the corner talking. I doubt she finds him and I'm sorry for her if she does. I continue on my search and see Brian and quickly turn and switch direction. I'm not ready to talk to him yet. *Where the hell is this girl?* I think ready to abort mission and go home and then I see her dancing her way toward me. She stops in front of me still dancing

"This is my song. How about that dance now?"

She doesn't wait for me to answer. She picks up my hand and I move in closer to dance with her. This is the first time I've taken the time to really look at Simone. She is beautiful. Her eyes have a beautiful sparkle. Maybe it's the strobe lights. I'll have to check under normal lighting but I'm pretty sure they sparkle. At least they do when we lock eyes. Her skin is as smooth as silk under my fingertips. As I rub up and down her arms my fingers tingle as if they've found where they belong, and her kiss gives me that first kiss sensation every single time.

After a few songs I go outside for some air. The party is packed and live and it's hot as hell in there. After a moment Trey joins me outside.

"Finally, up for air?" I ask referring to the make-out session I witnessed on my way out the door. He smiled.

"Yeah" he said with a chuckle. "Your girl Chantel is a trip. You know she thought she was going to make me leave Cheyenne in the corner and leave with her."

"I told you to leave her alone."

"No, you said not to deal with any of your friends. She's not your real friend. None of those girls are. Maybe Brianna but not the others." I shake my head. I know he's right but that has nothing to do with him and Chantel. I let it go and change the subject.

"You ready to go?" Just as I ask the question Simone comes outside.

"Yeah, let's roll". Trey said

"Why you leaving so early? Simone walked closer to me and picked up my hand.

"I'm just ready to go" I don't take my hand back.

"Y'all just got here" she whined. We didn't just get here. We all know that we've been here for quite some time. I don't contest. I just shrug again.

"Why don't you come back down here later? I could use some company while I clean this mess up." She's caressing my hand now.

"She's not going to be able to do that". Trey said pulling me away. "I'm sure she'll call you though."

I wave goodbye with one hand as Trey held tightly on to the other one pulling me in the direction of my house. Okay I said pulling my hand back when we were far enough away. Look he said before I could ask him what his problem was.

"No relationships right now ai'ight? You've had enough of that lately. It's time for a break from all-at. It's summertime. We're supposed to be summering."

"Summering?" I give a probing look.

"You know what I mean. It's the only time I can get you to do anything reckless, be an out-of-control teen.

"I am never out of control."

"Yeah a'ight."

"What's that supposed to mean?" I wrinkle my forehead

"You were pretty out of control back there", he said pointing backward.

"I was not" I slap his arm.

"Yeah right. If I didn't step in, you'd still be there" he said matter-of-factly

"Really? I suck my teeth and cut my eyes at him.

"Yeah, you'd probably be in her room by now."

"Boy, shut up."

"Nah I'm surprised she didn't kiss you goodbye. She was in lips reach after all."

"I-" That one I don't have a comeback for. I was surprised she didn't kiss me goodbye too. Now I'm wondering why she didn't kiss me goodbye.

"What's that look? Now you're wondering why she didn't kiss you goodbye aren't you?"

"No", I lie. He knows me way too well.

"I know you're going back over there tonight.

"Whatever", I shrug. "You act like I didn't see you making plans for tonight", I shake my head, "hater".

"Hater?"

"Yeah, you're a hater."

"I'm not a hater. I'm protecting you."

"From whom?"

"Girl, yourself. It's summer and I see how out of control you are".

"Oh, I see." I say smiling.

"What you see?" he raises his eyebrows.

"You miss me."

"I see you all the time" he said waving me off and looking down at his shoes.

"Yeah, but we haven't gotten into any trouble lately." He looked up and raised his eyebrows. We're usually both grounded by now and sneaking off to the lake house for the last weeks of summer.

"Exaaaactly. So now you see why I'm not for the relationship status right now. And the parentals are out of town. We should leave too"

I'm not sure what me being in a relationship has to do with anything.

"No. You just said the parentals are out of town. That means we can get into enough trouble here."

He thought for a second and said, "That is absolutely true".

"Yes it is. Now go forth and get into some trouble with Cheyenne and we can meet up here for breakfast".

"Word" he said hugging me and turning to leave. Before reaching the door, he turns and asks "Whatchu about to do?"

"We will talk about it over waffles." I turn him back around and lightly push him into the rest of his night. I text Simone inviting her to come by after her party. About an hour later I was watching a movie and she texted back saying she is on the- way. I know her party is still going on, so I wonder why she's coming now. I go outside and sit on the porch to wait for her. She arrived five minutes later and sat beside me on the porch.

"You're here early" I say as she takes her seat.

"Yeah, I just needed a little break from the party. I'm not staying long."

"Oh" I say "so what's up? What brings you by?"

"You invited me" she chuckled.

"Yeah, to chill." I know I invited her to come *after* the party.

"Oh, you finished curving me?" She smiles.

"I don't curve you. I'm just not looking for a relationship right now."

"Yeah Okay." She raises her eyebrows and nods her head.

"I mean, I just got out of one."

"I feel you. I don't want to be in one either to be honest with you". I give her the side eye. "For real" she shrugs, "it's summertime."

"What does that have to do with anything?"

"It's hot. I'm in heat. I can't be held b"

"Don't" I hold my hand up in front of her face. "Not that excuse."

"Alright then why don't you want to be in one?" she stands up and stands in front of me forcing me to look up.

"I just told you."

"Yeah besides that."

"I don't like labels." She doesn't respond. "It's hard to put into words but I don't like the idea of relationships for me right now. I was trying something out with having boyfriend." I'm sure what I just said makes no sense. I look away from her and across the street and see that Brian's light is on.

"Did you find what you were looking for?"

"Yeah, confirmation that I don't like labels. They ruin everything"

"I feel you" she shrugs. "I gotta get back to my party before something happens. You still coming by later."

"Nah I'm in for the night. You can come back if you want to though." I tilt my head up to look at her again.

"You sure" she asks with a wrinkled forehead.

"I invited you back, didn't I?"

"Alright then" she shrugged and bent down and kissed my cheek. "I'll call and see if you're still up".

"Cool" I said. I watched her walk down the steps and let her get a few steps down the sidewalk before I said, "Hey Simone."

"What's up" she said turning and walking backwards.

"You should definitely come back." She smiled.

"I got you" she nodded and turned back around. I watched her walk until she was out of my eyesight. I stood up to go inside, but I decide I'm not ready and sit back down.

Chapter 26

"Rise and shine" Trey bursts into my room. He flings open the curtains and I'm blinded even behind closed eyes.

"How did you get into my house?" I ask pulling the blanket over my head.

"Shut up girl you know I have a key." He jumps on top of me, and I roll him over beside me. He pulls the blanket from over my head just enough to see my eyes. "Good morning" he kisses my forehead and rolls over onto his back. We lay there for a moment. "It is most definitely waffle time" he says staring up at the ceiling.

I sit up and look at him pulling the blanket all the way down revealing Simone beside me.

"What the fu-...is that Simone?" Simone still asleep awakens at the sound of her name and look around. "Oh it is definitely waffle time" he laughs looking back at me.

"Shut up"

"What does waffle time mean? Simone asks sitting up. We both look at her. She looks confused. You could see the light bulb appear on top of her head when she finally figures it out.

"I'm definitely not invited to stay for waffles" she says plopping back down on the pillow and looking up at the ceiling. She sighs. "Alright I'm out" she moves to get out of bed.

"Oh no you don't" Trey leaps across the bed to lay across the both of us. "You are definitely invited to waffles" he points at Simone.

"Oh no" she holds her hands up "I don't want waffles."

"You don't like waffles?" I looked at her.

"Oh, I love waffles" she turned to look at me "but neither of us wants waffles" she leaned in and gently kissed my lips.

"Yeah well, I'll call you for parfaits later", I try to hold back my laugh, but she laughed first, and I just couldn't. Trey looked back and forth from me to Simone and back at me.

"Please? Waffles?

"No" Simone says. "I gotta go she says looking at her phone and sliding out of bed. "See" I smile, "she has to go".

"Alright then" he says getting up. "I'll be downstairs in the kitchen."

"Oh I'm not making waffles" I say getting out of bed.

"Duh. You can't cook" he shook his head and chuckled "get yourself together" he left the room closing the door behind him.

~ ~ ~ ~ ~

"Alright spill."

"Spill what?"

"How Simone ended up in your bed this morning"

"Oh that's easy. She slept there last night." He just looks at me. He doesn't say anything. He raises his eyebrows.

"Ok we had a sleepover" I shrug and try to hold back a smile.

"Lorde, have mercy" he said closing his eyes. Please have mercy."

"Not in the mood?" I chuckle. "Our food hasn't come yet my bad. I'll wait." I try not to laugh when he looks at me but my laugh escapes. I cover my mouth with both hands. I take a deep breath to gather myself. "Told you we should've started with your night." He just looked at me and shook his head.

"You're having the time of your life right now aren't you?" My phone vibrates and I check it. My smile fades,

"Well, I was."

"What's wrong?"

"Nothing." My answer is as dry as a bone.

"That's Mike."

"How you know?"

"Come on princess. It's me baby. Why you ain't answer?"

"Because I'm busy", I snap. He raises his eyebrows. "Ok I'm just not ready to talk" I calm down.

"I thought you was good. Yall ain't friends?"

"Yeah, we are, and I am good."

"You don't seem good. You seem like your feelings are hurt. So, what's up?

"Sorry that took so long" the waitress said putting our food down in front of us. "Can I get you anything else?"

"No thank you" we said in unison. Trey smiled at her and the waitress blushed.

"What's your name again sweetheart?"

"Morgan" she couldn't contain her smile.

"Ok Morgan. My name is Trey and I just want you to know that you're doing a wonderful job."

"Just doing my job" she said. "Let me know if I can get you anything else" she said finally breaking away from Trey's eyes to look at me.

"Thank you, Morgan" I smile.

"No problem" she blushes again and hurry away from the table.

"You're so rude" he says.

"I was actually polite. I smiled at her and everything." I know he's back to the subject of me not answering the phone for Mike. Before he can say anything my phone rings again. I ignore the call again and a text message comes through. I see that it's Mike and I ignore it again. I look at Trey and I smile.

"So" He says. I can tell he's about to circle back around to the subject of Simone and I'm right.

"You ready to tell me about this morning? Or last night? Or last night into this morning. I cut my waffle and take a few bites before I start talking. I tell him everything. I start with the text messages and end with this morning's scene. I tell him everything leaving nothing out.

"Ok wow. Yeah. Wow. So. I mean. Wow." He's wearing a look of amazement and full of questions he's not sure he wants the answers to.

"Dude, you still have questions, don't you?" I shake my head in disbelief.

"First of all, you seem way more excited about Simone than you did Brian. So yes, I most certainly do have questions. I just don't know if I want to know the answers to them. At least not yet". He looks so confused. "I'm impressed. It's not often you leave me feeling this way.

"Amazed yet discombobulated." I chime.

"What? I don't know what that means but you do so Imma say yeah."

"Look it up" I chuckle. In the meantime, it's your turn. Now spill. Where did you end up last night?"

"So, surprisingly I saw Lola last night." Already I don't like what I'm hearing.

"Wait what? You were with Lola last night?"

"Nooooo no-no-no-no-no" he said seeing the disgusted look on my face. "Well yeah" he shrugs. I put my fork down, "but not like that" he said quickly trying to clear up what he was trying to say.

"So, what was it like then?"

"She was at the party last night".

"Let me guess. She saw us and decided to call you to ask about me."

"Kinda but not really. She didn't call me. I saw her"

"I do not want to hear about her. It's waffle time now waffle." Lola is no longer a part of my life and I fully intend to keep it that way and that includes in conversation.

"She's kind of a part of the waffle" he says closing his eyes tightly and turning his head to the side.

"That's not funny." I cut my eyes at him.

"Relax I'm just playing" he throws his hands up in surrender, fork in hand and a piece of waffle on the fork.

"Yeah ok. She's in heat just like everybody else is. It's summertime. If it's up to you then…

"Then what" he challenges me. I lean in and look him in the eyes.

"You let that bitch spontaneously combust."

"Damn Lorde you're ruthless" he smiles.

"Whatever" I shrug. "Anyway, you talking or not?"

"Alright I was with Cheyenne last night" his smile gets bigger.

"Shy Cheyenne?" I know they were making out at the party last night, but I didn't know she was giving it up.

"Oh, she's not as shy as you think" he winks.

"Nah" I shake my head, "she's not like that".

"Not for everybody but she is for me now."

"Oh damn. Well ok." My eyes got big, and my eyebrows raised. He described his evening in more detail than my imagination could keep up with. I didn't expect for him to be so detailed as he described his night.

"Well then" I say "talk about wow." We pay the check and leave. When we get outside Trey stops suddenly and then starts walking again.

"What's up?" I ask him.

"We are still summering right?" There's that word again. A word that's just going to get me in trouble. Summering already made me lose my virginity...twice. Maybe summering with Trey is actually safer than on my own. He saves me from myself.

"Oh yeah. Summer ain't over yet" I smile.

"Good" he sighed a breath of relief. "I thought you were about to flake on me". "Why?" my forehead wrinkles.

"Simone duh. After last night one or both of yall are in love" he laughed. Just when he said that I got a text from Simone. I smiled and responded. I was so glad Trey wasn't paying attention.

"I know you ain't talking about somebody being in love after last night.

"Please girl. You know I ain't in love with nobody but myself" Trey laughs.

"Yeah aight. So, what's up? You tryna get some people together and hit the lake house?"

"Oh yeah" he said rubbing his hands together with a look of mischief sparkling in his eyes. I don't know what he's up to, but I don't give it too much thought. He's always up to something.

"You inviting your girl?" He looks at me out of the corner of his eye.

"I didn't plan on it" I cut my eyes at him.

"Why not?"

We're not in the stay for waffles stage so I doubt it's a good idea to invite her to stay for waffles over several days."

"What stage are yall in?" He's still looking at me with a side-eye.

"We're just friends" I shrug. It's not a lie. We both made it clear that we aren't looking for a relationship and that's not what this is.

"I think you should invite her."

"Only if you invite Cheyenne."

"I can do that."

"I know you hate Demetri, but do you mind if I invite him too?"

"What are you up to?"

Trouble

"Nothing."

"You gon catch another body already?" he looked at me. "Don't be out here hoein'."

"Excuse me but don't slut shame me." I punch his arm. "Look in the mirror to do that.

"Ok so I'm not slut shaming you because I don't know what that even is. All I said is don't be out here hoein. Now I imagine that if you don't want to be slut shamed then don't let them still be in your bed in the morning" he shrugs.

"Trey, a hoe and a slut are the same thing." I say rolling my eyes and shaking my head.

"Oh" he said. "Then I'm right then" he shrugged. I could see his point. I did not mean for him to see Simone this morning. I also didn't think I'd see him so early.

"You know I'm right" he smirked. I sucked my teeth.

"Whatever" I roll my eyes. When we get back to my house my phone starts ringing again.

"Answer it" Trey says looking at my phone. I ignore it. "See, he shakes his finger at me "I knew you wasn't good. You're not good Lorde"

Chapter 27

"Everybody shut the fuck up my mom is calling". I wait for complete silence before I answer.

"Lil girl don't act like I don't know you're at the lake house" my mother's voice blared through the phone before I could even say hello. I put her on speaker. "Is Trey there too?"

"He fuckin' better be", Trey's mother yelled from the background.

"Yes ma'am, he's here".

"Who the hell told the two of you it was ok to be there?"

"Well, I figured since we have keys it would be cool". I knew it wasn't cool when we planned it.

"LORDE DON'T PLAY WITH ME", my mother yelled.

"Okay okay I'm sorry".

"Look" she said calming down, "yall can stay there just don't make me have to fly home early. If I have to fly home early, it's going to be your asses."

"And yes, that was plural. ASSES!" Trey's mother yelled again from the background.

"Yes ma'am" we said in unison.

"And don't have no whole bunch of company in my house either".

"Yes ma'am" we repeated.

"AND NO FUCKIN PARTIES WHILE WE'RE GONE!" Trey's mom's voice was clearer this time.

"Yes ma'am". The line was silent for a moment.

"You know" my mother broke the silence "I don't know what's gotten into you. I specifically told you to stay your ass home".

"Well technically"

"SHUT UP lil girl don't you technically me."

"I'm sorry".

"Lorde, bye I'll call and check on you later".

"Bye mom".

"Bye god mommy" Trey yelled from across the room.

"Alright" I look at Trey "we are clearly in trouble when they get back, so we better make this good".

"Well," he shrugged "turn the music back on and let's get this party started". When the party was in full swing Demetri shows up. I roll my wondering how he got an invite. I was hoping he did not show up, but, as luck would have it, here he is, now standing in front of me with his arms open for a hug. I don't want to be rude, so I hug him. Now that I think of it, I did invite the boy.

"Didn't think you would make it."

"I told you I would. I wanted to see you. I ain't seen you since you started dating your boy. Where he at? he asked looking around. Demetri pops up every now and again, but he has no idea what's actually going on in my life. I think he just likes to be a fixture in it.

"He's not here". I don't offer any more details.

"What? He ain't your man no more?"

"Nah we ain't together no more". I shifted my weight to one side and tilt my head.

"Oh really? Forreal. Oh, then I can just", he wrapped his arms around me and picked me up by my butt. I wrap my legs around him. He kisses me. When we come up for air, I pat his chest with both hands. He gets that I want to be put down.

"Well," I say when my feet hit the floor. I clear my throat. "I guess you could do that, but the real question is do I want you to just do that."

"Oh shit I'm sorry. I can't take it back, but how do you feel about it now?" he smiles. *Boys really are dumb* I shake my head.

"Well, it felt good, but I don't like it. You're not exactly who I want it from."

"Seriously?"

"Look, you weren't willing to shoot your shot when I showed you I was interested. You couldn't even be honest with me. You just disappeared."

"True but I'm trying to redeem myself."

"Yeah" I shrug "but you can't. I mean don't get me wrong you are a superb kisser. Like really superb" I almost lose my thought, but I catch myself. "But I've already determined that I don't like you."

"So why did you invite me?" He looks unfazed.

"Honestly it was an accident. I figured it would be enough people here that it wouldn't matter".

"No you didn't" he said still unfazed. "But you know what? Imma head out". He leaned down and kissed my cheek and for no reason at all I pouted.

"But I'm not ready for you to go. He kissed my lips and took a step back. He looked at me for a second

"Then don't be so difficult." He stroked my face with the side of his finger.

"Come on" I pull his arm and lead him to the backyard. We walk toward the lake.

"I don't swim" he jokes.

"Relax there are chairs down here".

"So why you bring me down here? he asked as we sat down.

"To talk."

"We could've talked up there" he pointed toward the house. I got up and turned my chair to face his and sat back down in front of him.

"Ok well we can go back and enjoy the party, or we can stay here, and you can trust that I'm not going to drown you." He doesn't answer he just looks at me. "You want your chance at redemption, don't you?" I smack my legs.

"Yeah, I just want redeem myself I told you that's why I came

"Ok" I lean forward. "How do you plan to do it?"

"Well, I figured we could start over."

"Ok but you've already kissed me and that's not exactly starting" over I smirk. He chuckled.

"Ok so not all the way over then."

"So where do you want to start from?"

"How about we start with getting to know one another? We never really got the chance to do that". I raise my eyebrows but don't say what I'm thinking.

"Ok" I say. "So, tell me a little about yourself."

"What do you want to know?"

"Well considering all I really know about you is your name and that you'r e a good kisser, you can pretty much start where you want."

"Come on" he says, "don't do me like that. You know more about me than that". Again, I didn't say what I am thinking.

"You're right. I also know that you're kind of cute." I decided to stop giving him such a hard time. It made the conversation go much smoother. We talked so long we practically know each other's life story. I put my legs up with my feet on his lap and Demetri rubs my leg. I notice movement behind him. It's Trey walking toward us.

"Lorde we gotta clean up". I look at him. "Like now". I continue looking at him and say nothing. "Lorde, remember when your mom said don't make her fly home?" My eyes widen.

"What the hell happened in there?" I look toward the house and the party is still happening.

"Oh no everything is cool in there". Everybody is about to leave for the night except" he stopped and looked at Demetri.

"Ok" I say getting the hint and not letting him finish.

"That's my cue to leave" Demetri says taking Trey's hint.

"Sorry man" he said looking at me and shrugging.

"Ok um yeah I'll talk to you later Demetri." We stood up and hugged and he left.

"What happened for my mom to be coming home? Oh nothing. I just needed to get rid of your boy".

"Why?"

"Because Brian just showed up and I don't want any awkwardness or drama at this party. Now say thank you Trey". I take a deep breath

"Thank you Trey my ass. I've been avoiding Brian."

"Well now it's time to stop and face him. He thinks he did something wrong. He keeps asking me if you've said anything."

"He didn't do anything wrong."

"Don't tell me tell him" Trey says with a shrug just as Brian walks out the back door.

"Hey stranger" he says with a smile and opening his arms for a hug.

"Hey" I reply. I didn't plan to do this now but thanks to Trey here I am. "Let's dance" I say in an attempt to put this talk off for just a little bit longer. Thankfully he agrees and we head inside to dance. We got through one dance before the music slows down and he pulls me in closer to him. I feel someone grab me from behind. I see Brian's eyes widen. *It must be Simone.* I turn, Brian's arms still around my waist, and Simone is smiling and swaying back and forth.

"I've been looking for you."

"Hey, you found me." I smile back at her. She's looking at Brian who still hasn't let me go. "What's up?" I say gently pulling her face in to look eye to eye. When she adjusts her eyes back to me, I smile again. "You saving me a dance?" I ask flirtatiously.

"Yeah, I was coming to claim it now." There it is. That twinkle in her eye I was talking about. I want to stop dancing with Brian immediately, but I don't. Instead, I shake my head no. I place one hand on her hip.

"Not right now" I lean into her ear "I can't right now." I sigh "but don't go nowhere". She looked at me suspiciously. I wink at her. She dances off in another direction and I turn back and face Brian who is looking very confused. I return his look and he straighten his face.

"So, what brings you out here?" I ask, finally breaking the ice. I know I didn't make the mistake of inviting Brian.

"Trey said y'all were throwing a party and invited me". *Of course it was Trey.* I didn't accept that as an answer because he obviously didn't just come to party.

"So, what brings you to the party?"

"You. I wanted to talk to you" he says pulling me in closer. I try to control my nervous breathing but it's difficult and I hope he can't tell. "I've been thinking about you for a long time. Wondering why you won't answer my calls or text." He sighs deeply and I can feel his breath from ear down my neck. Trying to figure out what I did wrong. When Trey told me about the party, I figured it would be the perfect time."

"You didn't do anything wrong" I manage between nervous breaths. *This song seems to last forever. Is it even the same one?* I can't focus with him being this close to me. My thoughts won't leave my mouth. I back away

"Let's go outside. I need some air" I say. He leads the way. Once we're outside he scoops me up and carry me down to the chairs by the water. He sits me down and then takes the seat next to me.

"Are you sure I didn't do anything wrong?" he looks out at the water.

"You didn't do anything wrong. I just freaked out. It was my first time and I freaked out. I saw blood and freaked out. I saw you naked and I freaked out. I realized I was naked, and I freaked out. I was freaking out the whole time. When you left me in the tub, I cried."

"Why?" his forehead wrinkled.

"I was freaking out" I chuckle and shrug. "You were a perfect gentleman" I reach over, squeeze his hand and let go. "I didn't answer your calls and texts because I didn't know what to say to you.

"Well, I wasn't calling for you to talk. I was calling to talk to you. I was freaking out too. It was my first time too."

"Really" I wrinkle my forehead

"Yeah. You are the first person I actually wanted to do it with. Want to do it with. When I saw the blood, I freaked out too. I had no idea that was going to happen. I thought I did something to you. Hurt you or something".

I can see the worry in his eyes, and I know what he's saying is true and genuine.

"I wanted to come here and let you know that I still like you. A lot." I don't answer so he keeps talking " I came to ask you to be my girlfriend".

"I can't be your girlfriend."

"Why not?"

"Well I've decided that I don't do labels. Also," I shug "I kind of have something going on with Simone right now. She's not my girlfriend or anything but I know you want to be exclusive."

"I don't know what most of that even means right now but I think I heard no so I'll go with that. Whatever you have with Simone doesn't make me like you any less. You don't have to be my girlfriend, but I would still like to be uh- whatever this is. Friends I guess." I think about it for a moment and agree. Trey comes back out and finds me by the lake again. He lets me know that the party is over and everyone else is gone except Simone and Cheyenne. When I ask him why they stayed he just shrugs.

"Ok well, Simone isn't my girlfriend".

"Well you invited your not girlfriend to your lake house for the weekend." I didn't invite her to stay for the weekend, but I did tell her to not go anywhere. *Damn*

"I'll talk to her". Good luck he says as we walk through the door. Trey walks straight up to Cheyenne who is cleaning up cups and trash from the floor. Simone is cleaning up the tables and counters and in no time the house was clean. I lead Brian to the couch. When she finishes Simone joins us on the couch. Trey and Cheyenne join us moments later and we all talk until we fall asleep on the couch.

When I wake up Brian is gone, and Simone is in the kitchen cooking breakfast. I don't see Trey and Cheyenne, so I assume they're in one of the rooms. When I walk into the kitchen Simone looks up from what she's doing.

"Well, hello there" she says and turns her attention back to what she was doing.

"Hey" I say walking over and standing beside her. She just keeps doing what she's doing. I watch for a moment then I kiss her cheek and leave her side to go shower. When I return, she's finished cooking but she's still standing in front of the counter. I approach her from behind and I wrap my arms around her. She turned around to face me.

"I know we're not together but don't do that shit again. I don't do disrespect". She's referring to last night. I take her face in my hands and kiss her.

"I'm sorry" I say before releasing her face and grabbing onto her waist.

"Yeah. You better be. You hungry?" she asks. I back away a little and look her up and down.

"Don't ask me that". She smiles and jumps up onto an empty space on the counter.

"You hungry?" She repeats.

"We are starved" Trey comes in carrying Cheyenne on his back. Simone snaps her legs shut and jumps down off of the counter.

"Don't stop on our account". He says noticing how nervous she looked when she jumped down.

"Yeah, I'm always down for a good show" Cheyenne chimes in. Both Trey and Simone give her a shocked look.

"I like this one" I said laughing and pointing in her direction.

"Well, everything is laid out for you two so dig in. Here is your plate Lorde", Simone handed me a plate and picked up another off of the counter. "We'll just take our plates and go".

"Sorry" Trey said grabbing our plates. "We don't flee during waffle time."

"I didn't even make waffles." Simone looked confused.

"No. That's not why we call it waffle time remember?" I turn to Trey "and we don't usually share our waffles." Cheyenne looked back and forth between us.

"What are you two going to do after we graduate?" We both look at her.

"Go to the same college" Trey says and looks back at me. "You won this round, but you and I need to talk about some things."

"This is true. But first I have some things I need to do" I say picking up Simone's plate and handing it back to her and then picking up my own. I wink at Trey.

"We will see you two for lunch" I say and I take Simone's hand and lead her out of the kitchen. As soon as we get to the room. Mike calls. Simone looks at me like she wants to know who's calling. I don't answer. Mike and I decided that even though we aren't dating and won't be again we can still be friends. We were really good as friends and we didn't want to lose that. It took me a while to get over being mad at him, but we're cool now. He calls back and I answer.

"Hey Mike, what's up?"

"What's up I didn't get the chance to call you last night It got a little crazy". I had forgotten all about talking to him last night, so I wasn't upset.

"Oh really? What happened?" While I listened to Mike tell me about college life Simone grows restless and comes and sits on my lap. When I don't respond she turns and straddles me.

"What's been up with you?" He asks just as she does.

"Oh ok ooh", I say as she takes her shirt off.

"Ooh what?" Mike asks

"Simone" I answer unable to take my eyes off of her.

"Simone? The same Simone that kept kissing you?"

"Yeah."

"Oh, you kissin' her back now?

"Yup".

"I knew it" he said. He couldn't mask his excitement if he tried. Simone gets up and stand in front of me. I reach for her, but she moves back so I can't touch. I roll the chair closer, and she steps back again. I know he wants to know more but I don't have time for that right now.

"Mike let me call you back babes". I didn't wait for an answer before I hung up the phone and stood up.

"Come back here with my breakfast." I smile.

"You could've stayed seated for that because it was right behind you".

"Nah it's right here in front of me". She jumps on the bed and gets off on the other side.

"Alright" I raise my hands in surrender "I'm not going to chase you". I sit back down in my chair and pick up my plate. She stands in front of me with her hands on her hips. I look up to see a mischievous smile on her face.

"Don't play with my food unless you want to become a meal" I smile.

"So, what's up with you and Brian" she asks. My smile fades. This is not what I had in mind when we brought breakfast to the room.

After breakfast we shower and lie in the bed talking for a while. When I hear my stomach growl we head to the kitchen to see what Trey and Cheyenne are up to.

"Something smells" good Simone says as we enter. Nothing is cooking so I know she's being sarcastic.

"Relax. Lunch is on the way. We can't cook" Trey said.

"I can. I just didn't feel like it." Cheyenne said with a raised hand.

"On a scale from one to ten how much trouble do you think we're in? Trey asked. He doesn't look too concerned, but I know he is.

"Like I said we better make it good."

"What? Like regular good or end of the summer good?" I look at Cheyenne and then Simone out of the corner of my eye and back to Trey.

"We better make this end of the summer good. They're pretty pissed off."

He looked from Simone to Cheyenne and back at me. "And I'm going to get in trouble for both of them".

"No you won't, just one" I try to sound optimistic.

"Yeah right Lorde, you ready to come out to your parents?"

"Yeah" I shrug.

"And what would you be coming out as?" I hadn't thought about that. What would I be coming out as?

"We're definitely going to be grounded for at least two weeks" he says shaking his head.

"Nooo that's the rest of the summer you can't be grounded for my birthday. We have to fix this."

"Fix this?" I laugh. You heard my mother. Hell, and his. There is no fixing this. We have to just live it up while we have the chance and not give them a reason to come back early." Cheyenne sits back and pout. This girl is really starting to get on my nerves. It is time for her to go.

"Don't worry. We'll be there" Trey said taking Cheyenne by the hand.

"For real? She said looking at him with what I assume is a face that makes him weak. He looks at me for approval. I roll my eyes and shake my head.

"Yeah, we will be there."

"You promise?"

"No" I said quickly. "No promises." Cheyenne turned and looked at me with a confused look. "No promises" I said.

"Yeah, I'm sorry but no promises" Trey says.

"Ok let's just get through the rest of the weekend" Simone interjects. "If they're alive on Monday then we can worry about your birthday party. Now, what's up for tonight?"

"Since it's just us let's just chill. Trey says.

"Oooh let's do a bonfire" Cheyenne says clapping.

"Absolutely not. We are not setting any fires." Simone sounds irritated and her face matches her voice.

"Dang girl first you're crying about your birthday party now you want to do something that could further jeopardize your boy from going. You gotta chill girl."

We settled on watching movies. After the first one Simone decided that she didn't want to be around when my parents came back. I told her to at least stay the night, but she didn't want to risk it. She explained that she was thinking about what Trey said earlier about coming out. She said she isn't out to her parents and she didn't expect me to be or for Trey to take the fall for her. I knew I liked her for a reason. When she said she didn't want complicated she was serious She tried to convince Cheyenne to go home too but Cheyenne refused. I knew we were in trouble when she said

"I came with Trey and I'm leaving with Trey." If looks could kill, my best friend would be on his death bed with the way I'm looking at him. Cheyenne would be too if she saw how Trey was looking at her. After a while Simone announces that her ride is here and she's leaving. She offers Cheyenne a ride one last time and leaves after she refuses. I ask to borrow Trey for a moment and drag him into one of the rooms and close the door.

"She has to go" I whisper loudly.

"I know but what do you want me to do?"

"You're going to have to convince her to go home or we're dead".

"She has until tomorrow" he shrugs.

"Do you really think she's going anywhere tomorrow unless it's with you? He paces back and forth in thought.

"I have an idea. We can say"

"No, we can't say anything because they're not going to believe it. She has to go. You need to get rid of her."

"How?" he said panicking.

"I don't know Trey. How did you get her here?"

"How did you get Simone to leave?" he asked in a panic

"Simone is not my girlfriend. I haven't been carrying it like she is. She went home because she gets it. I let shit get boring for a reason and she got the hint."

"Well, can you throw some hints at Cheyenne?"

"No dumbass" I punch his arm "I can't because the only hint she's going to get while you're rubbing her between her thighs is that that's where you want to be. She's not going anywhere after you've been giving her the D all day and ready to go again".

"Don't hate the playa" he smiled.

"Focus" I yelled in a whisper. "She has to go. If I have to do it trust me when I say that she will stay away."

"You're so rude" he says shaking his head.

"No, you're so rude. I can show you rude" I said giving a mischievous smile.

"No thank you I got it" he said aggressively in a whisper. I kick him out of the room and call Mike. I need some guidance.

"I didn't think I'd hear from you again today" he answered his phone.

"Why?" I ask already knowing the answer.

"Simone seemed to be keeping you pretty busy."

"Nah she was chillin'" I said. There was two seconds of radio silence before we both burst into laughter.

"What's up Goddess?" He said after we regained our composure. "You can't get her to leave, can you?"

"It's not her" I sigh.

"Someone else?"

"Yes" I sigh again.

"What do you have going on over there? What kind of party did I miss?" he chuckles.

"Trust me these last two days have been pretty interesting. Trey invited this girl named Cheyenne and now we can't get her to leave without him. I don't know what to do because our parents are going to be home tomorrow".

"What time?"

"We don't know".

"Then just take her home." He said it like it was simple common sense.

"Yeah, but neither of us drive."

"Lorde get out of panic mode. You're smarter than this. How did yall get there?"

"Oh" I said having a lightbulb moment. "The only problem is that our parents told us to stay put. I'm already in trouble I don't need it to rain hell fire. We're already in trouble for being here when we aren't supposed to be".

"Lorde. Goddess" he was getting impatient. "Get the girl home and go back to the lake house so you don't have to worry about that. The worst you have to worry about is your parents seeing the charges for a car service."

"Yes! That's a much better plan than I had in mind."

"Do I even want to know what you had in mind?"

"It's probably best that you don't. it'll make for a good story if I ever have to use it."

We got in so much trouble for being at the lake house. We didn't know that they had cameras installed after the last time we snuck out there. Our parents saw everything. Not only did they see the party, they saw everything done in the common areas. We learned while getting in trouble that the bathroom and the bedrooms are the only places without cameras. They showed us the footage and we knew we were doomed for these last days of summer. We couldn't even talk our way out of it.

The End.

www.ingramcontent.com/pod-product-compliance
Lightning Source LLC
Chambersburg PA
CBHW070501260626
47161CB00004B/1404